Ever since their boyhood days, fifteen-year-old Jesse has craved something more than friendship from Kevin Corrigan. Athletic, handsome and cocky, Kevin doesn't seem approachable. But when Kevin spends a summer at Jesse's family's beach home, an affair ignites between them, one so intense it engulfs both boys in an emotional tug of war neither wants to give up on.

Published by
NineStar Press
PO Box 91792
Albuquerque, New Mexico, 87199
www.ninestarpress.com

Warning: This book contains sexual content, which is only suitable for mature readers.

Print ISBN # 978-1-947139-28-2
Cover by Natasha Snow
Edited by Jason Bradley

Kevin Corrigan and Me

Jere' M. Fishback

Chapter One

KEVIN CORRIGAN DIED two days ago, on a Thursday, at the age of sixty-five. I know this only because I saw his obituary in this morning's *Tampa Bay Times*. The obit provided limited information: date of birth, date of death, and Kevin's place of residence, Madeira Beach. It also said Kevin had no known survivors, but that isn't really true because I'm still alive and I am very much Kevin's survivor.

My name is Jesse Lockhart. I grew up in the Jungle area of west St. Petersburg, Florida, in a cinder-block home with a fireplace, casement windows, a weed-and-dirt yard, no air-conditioning, and an ineffective furnace. My parents divorced when I was six years old and my father disappeared shortly after that, so he wasn't a factor in my life. I lived with my mother and younger sister, Lisa.

Kevin was an only child who lived next door to me with his Boston Irish parents. He was a year older than me, and between my parents' divorce and the time I reached the age of eleven, Kevin became my primary masculine influence.

I worshipped him.

Always half a head taller than me, Kevin was lanky, with curly blond hair and a riot of freckles dancing across his turned-up nose. His blue eyes twinkled, and he was athletic in a way I would never be. He had a cocky attitude; he wasn't intimidated by anything or anybody, not snarling dogs, rattlesnakes, teenagers, or any type of authority figure: cops, umpires, or the nuns that taught at his Catholic primary school.

Okay, he wasn't the sharpest when it came to his schoolwork. I was mostly a straight-A student while Kevin scraped by with Cs, and every time report cards issued, his mom compared mine to his. Then she'd say to Kevin, "Why can't you be more like Jesse?"

But Kevin wasn't meant for school and textbooks; he wasn't designed to perform academic tasks. His world was the palmetto and pine forest near our homes, the baseball diamonds in our part of town, a tree house he built for himself, and the streets and alleys of our suburban neighborhood.

It seems hard for me to believe now, but when I was eight and Kevin nine, he and I often rode a city bus, unaccompanied by an adult, from the Jungle all the way to downtown St. Petersburg, a ten-mile journey, just to see a matinee at the Florida Theater. Afterward, we'd visit a magic shop called Sone's, a quirky place run by a Japanese couple where we bought stupid things to bring home: fake plastic puke, a whoopee cushion, and cigarette loads I snuck into my mom's Viceroys; they exploded with a bang shortly after she lit up. Once we bought a tin of itching powder, which I think was simply shredded fiberglass, and then on the bus ride home, Kevin surreptitiously sprinkled some of the powder down the backs of two women's sundresses, causing the women to writhe and scratch while we giggled and jabbed each other in the ribs.

Kevin's home life was a mess. His father, Colonel Frank Corrigan, was a wheelchair-bound WWII veteran who'd sustained spinal damage in the Pacific theater. He was in constant pain, and this caused him to be cranky and out of sorts. He puffed on Hav-A-Tampa cigars jammed into a holder he'd fashioned from a coat hanger because his fingers didn't work very well. He drove a black Cadillac with the accelerator and brakes operated by calipers attached to the steering wheel. He was always yelling at Kevin for one thing or another in a barking tone I could hear a block away. His favorite epithet was, "I'm gonna *kill* that kid, Margaret."

Margaret was Kevin's mother, the Corrigan household martyr who endured Kevin's mischievous behavior and her husband's unceasing demands. A bulky woman with auburn hair and a narrow, thin-lipped mouth, she bathed the Colonel, helped him in and out of bed, got him dressed, and cooked the family meals. She washed clothes in an old-fashioned ringer-style washtub, then hung them to dry on a clothesline in the Corrigans' backyard. She always seemed tired and dispirited to me. I rarely heard her laugh, and I often wondered whether the Colonel and Margaret had once enjoyed a happy marriage, back when the Colonel was healthy and Kevin wasn't part of their lives.

The Corrigans' social life revolved around the Madeira Beach Moose Lodge, the VFW, and St. Jude Catholic Church. Every Sunday they piled into their Cadillac to attend Mass with the Colonel's wheelchair loaded into the trunk by his wife. Once I went with them; I was curious to see how a Catholic service might differ from those at my Methodist church. Much to my surprise, the St. Jude Mass was conducted in Latin; I couldn't understand a word the priest said. Money was collected from parishioners through use of a metal basket attached to a telescoping aluminum pole operated by an usher. The day I was there, Kevin pretended to put money in the basket, but instead he stole a dollar when his folks weren't watching, then stuffed it into his pocket after giving me a wink. I felt appalled by his behavior, but of course I didn't snitch; I wouldn't have dreamt of it.

Kevin was a natural athlete; he could play any sport—baseball, basketball, or football—with agility and grace. But he couldn't get along with other players; he constantly got into scraps with members of opposing teams, or even with his own teammates. He had a way of needling guys with sarcastic remarks about their lack of athletic prowess or even their looks. ("Is that your nose or are you eating a banana?") In fact, he seemed incapable of forming true friendships with anyone other than me.

For reasons I didn't understand at the time, Kevin was drawn to me just as I was drawn to him. He never teased or threatened or taunted me like he did other boys in the neighborhood. He never called me an insulting nickname. I was by nature a gentle boy who lacked self-confidence in the masculine world, so I never tried emulating Kevin's miscreant behaviors on my own, but I loved serving as his sidekick and sycophant. I relished my role as abettor.

Many of our neighbors had citrus trees in their backyards: oranges, tangerines, and grapefruits. One night, at Kevin's suggestion, we snuck into the neighbors' properties to fill two paper grocery sacks full of grapefruits larger than softballs. Across the street from my house, a huge live oak grew in the right-of-way. One of the oak's limbs stretched across the road like an arm reaching for a box of crackers in the cupboard. Toting our sacks of grapefruits, Kevin and I scaled the tree and perched ourselves on the limb overlooking the road. When a car passed beneath us, Kevin or I dropped a grapefruit on the car's windshield, which always scared the bejeezus out of the car's occupants. Women screamed and brakes squealed. Men cursed. But of course no one could see us up there in the darkness.

Every Halloween Kevin and I dressed as hobos. We scavenged the neighborhood, collecting candy in our pillowcases while pulling the occasional prank. My favorite was one where Kevin scooped up a pile of dog turds using a Sabal palm boot as a shovel. He dropped the turds on someone's doorstep, soaked them in lighter fluid, and set them on fire.

Then he rang the unsuspecting homeowner's doorbell. The result, of course, was never in doubt. The surprised resident stomped the fire out with his shoe, only to belatedly discover what sort of material flamed. Kevin and I hid in a nearby bush, watching and chuckling so hard I think I might have peed in my pants.

Kevin liked to spy on people at night, on weekends or during summers when we could stay out until nine or ten. We peeped on women undressing, on an old guy who picked his nose and ate the boogers, on a pair of men who slow-danced together in their underwear to Johnny Mathis records, on a high school boy who often pleasured himself while leafing through a girlie magazine. I, of course, had never seen such things before. Kevin's spying opened up a whole new world for me, one I knew I would never discuss with my mom or sister or anyone else. How could I possibly?

I remember one summer when the Colonel traded in his Cadillac for a two-toned, cinnamon-and-cream Rambler station wagon. The Corrigans took a month-long cross-country trip in the Rambler, all the way to California, where Kevin sent me a postcard from Disneyland. He sent me another from the Alamo in San Antonio. Both were places I'd always dreamed of visiting, but figured I'd never see. That was a miserable month for me. I felt jealous of Kevin's travels and as lonely as I'd ever been in my young life. I think I was nine then. Of course there were other boys in the neighborhood and I did my best to pass the time with them, but it wasn't the same as being with Kevin. I longed for the day the Corrigans would return.

The Corrigans' house stood north of ours. Kevin's bedroom was at the southwest corner, while my bedroom was at the northwest corner of *our* house, so Kevin and I always slept about twenty feet apart. If we'd wanted to, we could have tossed a football back and forth between our bedroom windows. But I never spent the night with Kevin and he never spent the night with me because Kevin was a chronic bed-wetter. His mother kept a fitted rubber sheet on his mattress at all times, and this went on for as long as Kevin lived next door. I didn't know anything about the reasons behind bed-wetting, but even then I suspected it was caused by emotional distress of one sort or another, probably linked to his poor school grades, his father's withering tirades, and the Colonel's very obvious disability that surely must have embarrassed Kevin. But I always kept his bed-wetting problem to myself; I never even mentioned it to my mother or sister. I figured I owed it to Kevin to keep his habit a secret from the rest of the world.

When Kevin and I were boys, Catholics were not supposed to eat meat of any sort on Fridays: no beef, chicken, or pork. So every Friday Mrs. Corrigan prepared a dinner featuring Mrs. Paul's fish sticks. These were tasteless little rectangles of processed and frozen cod you heated up on a cookie sheet, and Kevin detested them.

"They taste like cardboard," he told me, "even when I cover them with tartar sauce."

At *our* house, my mom prepared a fried chicken dinner every Friday—the tasty meal was a ritual—and every Friday Kevin would sneak over to our house to dine on fried chicken, unbeknownst to his parents. Of course, my mom knew what was up, but she never told Kevin's parents he violated God's law every Friday night. She let him gnaw on wings and legs with abandon because Mom was that way. Within reason, she believed in giving kids the freedom to do whatever they chose.

The summer before my sixth-grade year, I was nearly eleven and Kevin was already twelve. He was almost as tall as my mom at that point—he'd put some muscle onto his frame as well—and I remember very clearly an incident involving Kevin, a truly cathartic experience for me. I had just finished my breakfast and brushed my teeth, and I walked over to the Corrigans' house to see what Kevin was up to. Their garage door was open, and I heard someone rattling about inside, so I walked into the garage's shadowy interior where I found Kevin rummaging through the contents of a cardboard box. He wore nothing but a flimsy pair of briefs that clung to his buttocks and displayed a randy bulge in front.

Kevin might as well have been naked.

Right away my mouth grew sticky and my knees wobbled. I lived with two females—I had never seen another boy in his underwear—and the sight of Kevin's lean physique captivated me in a strange way I hadn't felt before. There in the garage, I thought Kevin was the most beautiful thing I'd ever seen. I felt so stunned I couldn't speak. I just clenched and unclenched my fingers at my hips while I kept my gaze focused on Kevin.

When he finally noticed me standing there, Kevin gazed at me with his eyes narrowed and his forehead crinkled, as if to say, "What are *you* looking at?"

It was then, of course, I realized something about myself that I'd never before suspected: I felt a *physical* attraction to Kevin; I wanted to touch him in ways that weren't allowed in the world we dwelt in, and the realization that I harbored these urges frightened me out of my wits. I didn't know what to do or say, so I turned on my heel and *ran* back to my house as quickly as I could. I went to my room and closed the door behind me. Then, after I sat on my bed, I rocked back and forth while wagging my knees and cracking my knuckles. My stomach roiled and my heart thumped. Between my legs, I felt a stiffening as I recalled exactly what I'd seen in the Corrigans' garage. My viewing of an almost nude Kevin had seared his sex appeal into my brain, and I was never quite the same guy after that morning. There in my bedroom, I knew I was somehow different than other boys, and though I couldn't yet articulate *how* I was different, I was certainly on my way to finding out. Neither Kevin nor I ever mentioned the incident in the garage after it happened. In fact I suspect Kevin had no idea what it had meant to me or how that moment had altered my view of myself.

But I knew.

About halfway through that summer, something even *more* earth-shattering occurred: the Corrigans decided to move out of their house next to mine and into a newly built three-bedroom home in the community of Largo, Florida, in central Pinellas County. The new home was probably ten miles from the Jungle, but it might as well have been a thousand, and when Kevin told me of the impending move, I felt as though a trap door had opened up beneath me. Kevin and I were fishing on the Jungle Prada Pier when he broke the news, and he didn't seem the least bit sad about the move. The new home, he said, had a screened-in swimming pool, plus it was much larger and far more modern than his present home.

There on the pier I wanted to cry, but of course I didn't let myself, not until I got home from fishing. I can remember going to my room that afternoon and closing the door. I lay on my bed and wept like I never had before. My shoulders shook and my lungs pumped while I soaked my pillow in tears. I felt like someone was ripping my guts out of my body, one handful at a time.

There would be no more Kevin: no more peeping, no more clandestine chicken-eating on Friday nights, no more Halloweens with Kevin, and no more bus rides into the city. It was all over, just like that, and I felt betrayed and cheated. It seemed so unfair. What was wrong with the house the Corrigans already owned? And why wasn't Kevin sad about leaving me behind? Did I mean so little to him? Did he not have the same feelings for me that I felt for him?

Oh, I told myself, *he's not like me, is he?*

The move seemed to happen overnight, and then a For Sale sign from a real estate office went up in the Corrigans' front yard. For days afterward, I walked around my home like a zombie. I'd gaze out my bedroom window at Kevin's old bedroom window and wonder what Kevin was doing just then. Had he found a new sidekick to replace me in his new neighborhood?

My mom took me to visit the Corrigans a time or two, shortly after they moved. Their new house stood on a treeless lot surrounded by other homes that pretty much looked the same: one-story structures with stucco-over-cinder-block walls, aluminum-framed awning windows, and two-car garages. The whole neighborhood was built on a bulldozed orange grove. To me the Corrigans' new house seemed cold and lifeless with its large rooms and terrazzo floors. I swam in the pool with Kevin during those visits—there were two, I believe—but I didn't enjoy myself. I think I instinctively knew that the sooner I put Kevin out of my life, the better off I'd be because Kevin's temporary presence pained me more than I could say.

I had to move on.

A few years passed, during which we moved from the Jungle to a cottage on Treasure Island, a beach community a few miles away. The Gulf of Mexico wasn't more than one hundred yards from our front door, and this opened up a whole new world for me. I could spend hours at the beach. I could fish at the John's Pass Bridge or go pool-hopping in the numerous motels that lined the shore.

Kevin, of course, made no attempt to stay in touch with me. We received a Christmas card each year from the Corrigans, and that was about it. Kevin, I assumed, had forgotten about me and I had pretty much forgotten him, but then something unexpected happened to change all that.

Chapter Two

DAYS AFTER MY ninth-grade school year ended—it was the last summer I didn't work full-time—Kevin's mom phoned mine to ask a favor. Mrs. Corrigan was scheduled for heavy-duty surgery requiring ten weeks of convalescence. She would place the Colonel in a nursing home during that period, but she didn't know what to do with Kevin. Was it possible Kevin could live with us? If so, Kevin's mom said, the Corrigans would give my mom a check to cover the extra food and incidentals Kevin would consume during his stay.

When Mom raised the question with me, I wasn't sure what to say. My first thought was, *I wonder if he's still a bed-wetter*, but that wasn't my main concern. I didn't really *know* Kevin any longer. What was he like now? If I said yes, then I'd share my bedroom with Kevin and likely spend every day with him during his ten-week stay. What if we didn't get along?

Still...

Despite the abrupt ending of our friendship and Kevin's lack of communication over the past three years, I still felt a sense of loyalty to him. If I said no, I would hurt his feelings. And I wanted to help Mrs. Corrigan with her dilemma. She'd always been kind to me. Shouldn't I do something to help her?

So I told my mom, "Sure, it's fine. Kevin can share my room with me," and a week later, Kevin arrived with his things: clothes, shoes, a fishing rod, and a tackle box. Mrs. Corrigan brought Kevin to our house in the Rambler station wagon, which wasn't quite as shiny as it had been when they'd driven it to California. She looked pale and she'd lost a good deal of weight since I'd last seen her.

Kevin had changed as well. In fact, he didn't look the same at all, save for his wavy blond hair, twinkly blue eyes, and freckled nose. When he exited the Rambler, my heart skipped a beat. He was taller than his mother now. His shoulders were broad, his limbs sinewy. His calves and the tops of his feet were dusted with golden fuzz, and his voice had a rasp to it when he greeted my mom, my sister, and me with a smile that showed off his big teeth. His cheekbones were craggy, his chin square, and I immediately knew that the boy who'd shared life with me in the Jungle was gone. Kevin was well on his way toward manhood.

When he greeted me, we didn't shake hands. Instead Kevin hugged me and mussed my hair, and for the first time that summer, I smelled his skin. His body odor reminded me of the scent of wet pine needles. I, of course, hugged Kevin back. I threw my arms around his slender waist and squeezed.

Right there, in our sandy front yard, with the Rambler's engine ticking and afternoon sunlight reflecting off the car's chrome bumpers, all the distance between me and Kevin and all the resentment I'd felt toward him since he'd moved from the Jungle disappeared like a puff of smoke from a campfire. Kevin was there, holding me. I was holding him and everything was okay.

After the hug, Kevin looked me up and down. Then he said, "What've you been eating? You're as tall as me now."

During my ninth-grade year, I'd shot up nearly four inches. Now I was three inches shy of six feet, and I'd put a bit of muscle onto my frame as well. Light brown hair grew on my calves and other places, and peach fuzz dusted my upper lip. I was on my way to manhood too.

Mrs. Corrigan wagged a finger at Kevin while warning him of dire consequences should he misbehave in the coming weeks. Then she drove away with her muffler growling. I helped Kevin take his belongings to my room, all except the fishing pole and tackle box. Those went into our garage. Kevin stored his socks and underwear in a bureau drawer I'd cleared out for him; the rest of his clothes, along with his shoes, went into my closet. After I told him which bed was his, he sat on it with his forearms resting on his knees and his hands hanging.

"So," he said while his gaze traveled about the room, "what's a guy do for fun around here?"

I explained about the beach, fishing at the bridge, pool-hopping at Treasure Island's multitude of motels, and a mini-golf course within walking distance. "And there's a pinball machine at the Surf Motel," I added. "The cabana boy showed me how to play it for free by sticking the end of a coat hanger in the coin slot; it works every time."

"Any chicks in the neighborhood?" Kevin asked.

My mood plunged at his question, and I didn't know how to answer him because girls didn't interest me. "Maybe one or two," I answered, "but I don't know them."

Kevin nodded. Then he asked, "Do we have time to visit the beach before dinner?"

I glanced at the clock on top of my bureau. "Sure, 'cause we won't eat till six thirty."

I closed the bedroom door, and Kevin and I changed into our swim trunks. After three years of showering with my classmates in PE, I'd lost all sense of modesty and I guess Kevin had as well, since neither of us seemed uncomfortable about getting naked in front of the other guy. I'll admit I stole a few glances at Kevin's private areas when he dropped his briefs to his ankles, and what I saw made my mouth grow sticky. The thought we'd sleep in the same room for ten weeks had my pulse racing.

As always, the cries of seabirds and the Gulf's briny scent stirred my senses when we strolled toward the shore with our bare feet squeaking in the powdery sand. Overhead, the sun burned like a yellow coin in a cloudless sky. We both waded into the Gulf's warm and placid water till we were up to our waists in liquid, and then Kevin pointed westward to a sandbar that had risen above the waterline, about a quarter-mile out.

"Is that always there?" he asked.

I nodded. "It's up several hours at a time, whenever the tide's low."

"Let's pay a visit," Kevin said, and then we swam out there, both of us doing our personal versions of the front crawl. The water we swam in wasn't deep at all; we could have walked to the sandbar with our heads above water if we'd wanted to. But at our ages, we had boundless energy and preferred to swim. I wasn't even tired when we reached the sandbar, the crest of which was maybe two feet above the water surrounding it. When we crossed to the west side of the sandbar, Kevin whistled. Then he pointed to a wave maybe three feet high, rolling toward the bar. The wave's face was glassy and sunlight glistened in its curling lip.

"Do you get that kind of wave out here often?" he asked.

I bobbed my chin while I ran my fingers through my damp hair. "It's like a machine pumps them out. Sometimes I come out here to body surf. You can do it for hours if you want."

"Ever ride a surfboard?" Kevin asked.

I shook my head.

Kevin rubbed his chin with a knuckle while he kept his gaze fixed on another incoming wave, this one identical to the last. "I have a board at home, a Gordon & Smith. Think your mom would take us to my place so we could bring it here?"

"Sure," I said. "She wouldn't mind."

Kevin turned his gaze to me. Then he looked me over from my forehead to my feet, as though I were an item he pondered buying in a store. "I can teach you to ride," he said. "It's not easy—it takes practice—but you're built like a surfer. You'll pick it up fast, I think."

I felt heat in my cheeks when Kevin's gaze traveled over me a second time. Then I swung my gaze to the Gulf. I tried to imagine myself gliding across the face of a wave like the surfers in California I'd seen on TV. Could *I* possibly do it?

MY MOM WAS a good cook, and for Kevin's first dinner at our house, she breaded and fried fresh shrimp from a seafood market, accompanied by tartar sauce, french fries, and a tossed salad with Italian dressing. Our dining table was actually a Formica-clad door supported by four cast-iron legs. One of the longer sides of the table abutted the sill of our front windows. I sat at one short side of the table while my mom sat at the other. Kevin and Lisa occupied the two seats facing the windows. A nice breeze swept through the room while we dined and Kevin answered my mom's questions about his school.

Kevin attended Bishop Keating High School, a Catholic institution located only a short distance from our old Jungle neighborhood, and although the school's principal was a priest, most of the faculty members were laypeople.

"No more nuns in their penguin outfits," Kevin told us.

The conversation turned to sports. "I played safety on the JV football squad last year," Kevin said. "I'll try out for varsity this fall."

A vision of Kevin dashing across the gridiron in a helmet, shoulder pads, and cleated shoes entered my mind's eye, and just like always, I felt a twinge of jealousy. Why wasn't *I* gifted with athletic prowess? Would I always be an observer at sporting events instead of a participant?

When we'd finished our meal, my mom decreed Kevin and I would take on dishwashing responsibilities after dinner each night. My sister would handle breakfast and lunch dishes. Normally my sister and I divided these chores evenly, so Kevin's participation would only lighten our loads. I was fine with the arrangement, and if Kevin minded, he didn't let on. Minutes later, I stood at the sink with my hands in soapy water while Kevin dried glasses and put them away in the cupboard. Every so often, his hip nudged mine, and I'd feel a kind of sexual spark pass from Kevin to me.

For the tenth time since his arrival, I found myself wondering how it might feel to touch Kevin between his legs, but then I remembered how he'd asked if any "chicks" lived in my neighborhood, and I knew it wasn't likely my desire for Kevin would ever be satisfied.

Shit.

MY MOM DROVE a convertible, a British sedan that wasn't the most reliable of cars, but it usually got us where we needed to go, and three days after Kevin moved in with us, she took us to Kevin's house to retrieve his surfboard.

When we reached the Corrigans' house, the one with the swimming pool, I stayed in the car while Kevin let himself in the house with a key hidden under a flowerpot. I kept remembering the few times I'd visited Kevin there and how unhappy I felt when doing so, so I had no desire to go inside. Within moments, the automatic garage door opened with a creaking and clacking and Kevin emerged onto the driveway with his surfboard under an arm. The board was a mammoth thing, nearly nine feet long and about three inches thick, except where it thinned out at the nose and tail. It had a fiberglass finish over a foam core with a single fin in the rear and a wooden stringer running the length of the board. Sunlight reflected in the board's glossy finish, and in the red-and-white Gordon & Smith logo near the board's nose.

My mom lowered her convertible top, and Kevin wedged the board into the space between the driver's seat and the rear seat. After he closed up the house, Kevin hopped into the rear seat beside the board, and we hit the road. We drew curious glances from motorists on our trip back to Treasure Island. Surfboards weren't commonplace in Pinellas County back then because there weren't many spots in our area with waves big enough to ride. Kevin's board rose about four feet higher than the car's windshield, and I suppose we must've looked like a shark cruising its way along Gulf Boulevard.

A WEEK AFTER Kevin's arrival, the tides table ruled our lives, Kevin's and mine. We quickly learned that the best times for catching waves at the sandbar were the three hours on either side of low tide, and since each day, low tide came about forty to sixty minutes later than it had the day before, we had to alter our daily schedule to allow ourselves maximum surfing time.

It took me two days before I finally managed to catch a wave and stand up on the board for a ride toward shore. We had been on the water nearly three hours, and the time was about eleven a.m. We took turns using the board, and now Kevin sat on the shore while I perched on the board, looking westward and waiting for the next wave to come. When it did, I lay on my stomach with my chin above the Gordon & Smith logo. I paddled furiously, chopping at the water with my cupped hands. I heard the wave's roar behind me, then felt it lift me. After I gripped the board's rails, I pushed myself upward into a crouch with my right foot forward. For a moment, I thought I might lose my balance, as I had so many times before. But this time, using my arms to steady myself, I managed to keep my footing. I turned the board's nose to my left by shifting my hips and skimmed across the wave's face.

I felt weightless, like I was flying. I felt the sun's rays on my shoulders, heard the wind whisper in my ears. I gazed into the cloudless sky, then hollered like a banshee. I had never felt so alive or so free.

By the time I made it to shore, Kevin was on his feet, clapping his hands above his head and doing a war dance of sorts. After I walked the board onto the beach and laid it in the sand, Kevin took me in his arms and gave me a bear hug. I felt his body heat and smelled the salt crystals on his skin while he pounded my back and told me how great I'd looked riding the wave.

"You're a natural," he said. "What did I tell you?"

Non-athlete that I was, I found it all quite hard to believe.

I could surf?

Me?

Chapter Three

EVER SINCE WE moved to Treasure Island, I'd earned money by caring for neighbors' yards. I mowed and edged grass, trimmed hedges, and weeded plant beds. I spread fertilizer and mulch. The money was decent, and at the time Kevin moved in with us, I probably had $150 stashed in a zippered pouch I kept under my bed.

After my first successful surfboard ride, I spent a half hour each morning scouring the classified ads in the *St. Petersburg Times*, searching for a used board I could buy. I quickly found one I bought for $75 from a guy in Redington Shores, a nine-foot Velzy made in California that was dinged in several places but still serviceable. Again, we drew stares on Gulf Boulevard when my mom drove me, Kevin, and my new board back to Treasure Island with the Velzy sticking up from the car like a cowlick. But I didn't care about the staring. I was now an official member of the surfing fraternity, albeit a novice. I'd finally found a sport I could perform adequately in, and I promised myself I would dedicate the remainder of my summer to honing my wave-riding skills.

So Kevin and I spent a portion of each day at the sandbar, sometimes as long as six hours if we had enough daylight for it. When we weren't surfing, we pool-hopped, and I remember one late afternoon when we swam in the Thunderbird Hotel's pool, a mammoth thing surrounded by a concrete deck littered with chaises, tables, and chairs. Dozens of tourists lounged about the pool in their swimsuits. Their skins glistened with suntan lotion and their sunglasses reflected the hot sunshine pounding the pool deck.

At one point, Kevin and I rested our arms on the pool's ledge with our bodies submerged up to our chests. Our wet hair was plastered to our skulls and beads of pool water gleamed like opals on our shoulders.

Kevin leaned to me and whispered into my ear. "See that skinny guy lying on the chaise with the yellow towel?"

I looked at the man and nodded.

"I think he's gay," Kevin said. "He keeps staring at me when I'm on the diving board."

I crinkled my forehead. "What do you mean he's gay?"

Kevin looked at me like I was stupid. "It's a nice way of saying queer."

I looked at the man again. He didn't seem any different from half the other men present, at least not to me. "Are you sure?" I said.

"Positive. I know a gay man when I see one."

"How?" I asked. Already I felt both intrigued and uneasy. This was the first time Kevin had ever mentioned homosexuality to me, so we were navigating unchartered waters. Plus if Kevin could spot a gay man so easily, how long would it take him to figure my story out?

When Kevin hopped out of the pool, water sheeted off his limbs. Then he motioned me to join him. "Let's take a walk," he said, and I followed him to the shore, where we strolled northward, back toward my house. "I'm going to tell you something," Kevin said while we ambled along with our arms swinging, "but you have to keep it to yourself, understand?"

I nodded.

"About six months ago, my folks went to a movie downtown, one I didn't want to see, so they left me at the Pier a few hours."

The Pier was a St. Petersburg landmark jutting a quarter mile into Tampa Bay. People fished there, or they patronized shops in the Pier's three-story Mediterranean-style structure. The place was quite popular at the time; it drew huge crowds on weekends.

"I met this guy there," Kevin said. "I was sitting on a bench, and I noticed him staring at me. After a while, he sat down beside me, and we talked. He was old, like maybe thirty."

My scalp prickled while Kevin continued.

"After we talked a bit, he asked me if I'd ever had a blow job, and I said, 'No, what's that?' And he said, 'I want to suck your dick. We can go to my place; it's not far from here. I'll pay you ten dollars if you'll let me.'"

By that point, my pulse raced and my mouth was dry.

"What did you do?" I asked.

Kevin looked at me like I was nuts. "I said no, of course, but ever since, I've noticed how certain men stare at me. It's like they're trying to imagine how I'd look with my clothes off. Do you know what I'm saying?"

I nodded, but in truth, I *didn't* know, and I wondered if perhaps some men looked at *me* that way.

ONE NIGHT, ABOUT ten days into Kevin's stay, the two of us played mini-golf at a course several blocks from my house, the kind with a windmill, a loop-de-loop, a waterfall, and a clown's head with a mouth that opened and shut every few seconds. The weather was warm and breezy, and we both wore T-shirts, shorts, and rubber sandals. Traffic whizzed by on Gulf Boulevard while we played. The breeze stirred fronds on Sabal palms that dotted the course, and the fronds made a sound like cards being shuffled. Of course, Kevin was a better player than I; halfway through the round, he already had four strokes on me. We were at the tenth hole, getting ready to putt across a miniature version of the Brooklyn Bridge, when I pointed to a restaurant's parking lot just across the street. I told Kevin of a prank a neighbor boy and I liked to play on the parking valets at the restaurant. The valets, I told Kevin, were arrogant pricks, older high school boys who thought they were tough.

"When they take a guest's car keys," I said, "they always give the guest one half of a numbered ticket. Then they slide the other half of the ticket under the car's windshield wiper before they park the car. When a guest is ready to leave, he gives the valet the guest's half of the ticket, and then the valet matches the number with the one on the windshield, get it?"

Kevin nodded while he gazed at the restaurant parking lot and I continued.

"Sometimes at night, my friend and I sneak over there; we hide between the cars. Then, when the valets aren't around, we'll switch the tickets on different cars' windshields. We do it to six or eight cars, and then we come back over here to watch the fun. It's total chaos."

Kevin chuckled while I jerked a thumb toward the restaurant. "Want to give it a try when we're finished here?"

I figured Kevin would jump at the chance. It seemed exactly the sort of prank he might have cooked up back in our Jungle days. But right after he struck his ball with his putter, he looked up at me and shook his head.

"Why cause trouble for people?" he said. "I mean, what's it accomplishing?"

My jaw dropped at his response. What had happened to the rascally Kevin I'd known three years before?

Chapter Four

ON A FRIDAY night, my mom took my sister, Kevin, and me to a drive-in movie theater to watch an Elizabeth Taylor/Richard Burton film, *Who's Afraid of Virginia Woolf?*, a movie I neither understood nor cared to. To me, Taylor and Burton came across as a couple of drunks who detested each other *and* their shitty marriage. Kevin and I sat in the car's shadowy backseat, which was a fairly tight squeeze for two long-legged teenage boys, and because I was bored, I bounced my knees and cracked my knuckles. I drummed my fingers on the windowsill beside me until my mom turned and told me to quiet down, that I was disturbing her concentration on the movie.

I rolled my eyes and rocked my head against my seat back. I stared at the car's fabric roof while I crossed my arms at my chest. Would the movie never end? Why would anyone pay money to watch such drivel?

I can't wait to—

Kevin's knee touched mine. We both wore shorts, and I felt the warmth of his skin. Right away, my pulse accelerated. When I looked at Kevin from the corner of my eye, his gaze was fixed on the movie screen. His expression was impassive. We shared a box of buttered popcorn, and when he passed the box to me, seconds later, I placed it in my lap. I ate a few handfuls while I savored the feel of Kevin's skin against mine.

I wasn't quite sure what to make of the situation in the backseat. Was Kevin making a pass at me, or was he simply trying to relax his leg? I decided to take a chance, to make a subtle move, so I rubbed my knee up and down against Kevin's knee; I did this three times. Then I stopped and held my breath.

Seconds passed. Then Kevin rubbed me back: once, twice, three times. By the third rub, my heart hammered against my ribs and my breathing had quickened. I stole another glance at Kevin, but his gaze remained fixed on the movie screen as before. I returned my gaze to the movie as well, feeling totally confused. What was going on? Was my imagination running away with me?

It wasn't.

Kevin seized my wrist. He lifted my hand and brought it to his crotch, where something warm and rigid bulged beneath the flimsy fabric of his shorts. My eyes bugged; I swallowed noisily and trembled like a kid in a spook house. I'm sure Kevin felt the trembling because my knee chattered against his and my hand shook between his thighs.

I turned my head to look at Kevin, and this time he swung his gaze to meet mine. He gave me a wink, ever so subtly and placed his hand on mine that rested between his legs. He gave my hand a squeeze. Then he turned his gaze back to the movie. We sat like that for the duration of the film, probably forty-five minutes, and Kevin remained stiff the entire time. Of course I was stiff as well, so rigid I feared I might bust the zipper out of my shorts. But then the film ended, and after Kevin withdrew his hand from mine, I removed my hand from Kevin's crotch before my sister or mom could see what we were up to in the backseat.

My thoughts raced during the ride home. What had it all meant? Did Kevin want me the same way I wanted him? And what, if anything, would happen next?

Back at home an hour dragged by before my mom and sister decided they would turn in. Mom extinguished lights in the living room while Kevin and I headed to my room. After I closed and locked the door, we both undressed without saying a word to each other. I tried to imagine what sort of thoughts dwelled in Kevin's head as he slid beneath his bedcovers. I switched off the floor lamp that stood between our beds, then crawled into my bed. I lay on my back with my fingers interlaced behind my head and my elbows jutting. I listened to waves smack the nearby shore. I heard the breeze stir needles of an Australian pine outside my bedroom window. Tires hissed on asphalt when a car passed on Gulf Boulevard. After my eyes adjusted to the darkness, I turned my head to look at Kevin. He also lay on his back. One of his knees was raised beneath his covers and he rocked the knee from side to side.

Go on: say something.

"You awake?" I whispered.

Kevin turned his head to look at me. "Yeah, of course," he said. "I'm not really sleepy at all."

"I'm not either."

Kevin pulled aside his covers. He swung his feet to the floor, and his knees crackled when he rose. His erection tented the pouch of his white briefs. He came to my bed and sat on the edge of the mattress, close to my chest. Already I smelled his piney scent. He stroked my cheek with a fingertip a time or two. Then he ran his fingers through my hair while my heart chugged like a locomotive climbing a hill. After Kevin reached for the edge of my covers, he lifted them.

"Can I?" he whispered.

My voice croaked when I answered. "Hop in," I said.

What transpired during the next hour was nothing short of magical, at least for me. When our briefs came off and our bodies intertwined, I felt the heat of Kevin's flesh, the firmness of his muscles, the softness of his lips, and the wetness of his tongue. We did things I'd never thought of doing with boys, intimate acts that felt entirely natural and right. Toward the end, when Kevin thrust inside me and his warm breath blew into my ear, I shivered with an excitement so intense I nearly screamed. And when it was over, I lay on my sweat-soaked sheet, staring up at the tongue-in-groove ceiling while Kevin snored in the other bed. Even today, whenever I smell the coconut scent of a certain skin lotion we used that night, I'll remember my first time with Kevin as clearly as though the moment happened yesterday.

We didn't say more than two dozen words to each other during our sex. Mostly Kevin spoke, telling me what to do or how to do it or what he planned to do to me next. But I'd never felt closer to anyone. I thought back to that summer morning in the Corrigans' garage, when I'd first discovered my desire for Kevin's flesh, and I could not believe how events had led Kevin and me to this. My limbs felt like jelly. I ran my fingers through my damp hair while I marveled at the memory of Kevin's techniques, his tenderness, and also his creativity. Who knew that Kevin's tongue twirling in my ear could make my heart sing?

And now I knew something else: a place in the world existed where I belonged. My need for another male's touch might be deemed wrong in most quarters—I'd have to be careful who I shared those feelings with—but at least I knew I wasn't alone.

THE SURF MOTEL was only a few blocks from our house, and the night after our first sexual encounter, right after we'd finished doing the dinner dishes, Kevin and I strolled down Sunshine Lane, a graveled alley leading to the motel, where we'd play pinball. We passed beneath the glow from streetlamps, both of us wearing Bermuda shorts, T-shirts, and flip-flops. The evening breeze tossed Kevin's wavy hair about while it blew my bangs into my eyes.

We had risen that morning around eight. Kevin woke first, and his stirrings in the room woke me. When I turned onto my side to watch Kevin pull his swim trunks up his legs, his gaze met mine and gave me a wink like he had in the car the night before. The wink meant something, of course. It signaled me that our sex the previous night had not been a one-time thing. It also meant that now we shared a secret *and* a new bond between us.

As always, we had spent several hours surfing at the sandbar. By now our days on the water had left my skin as dark as alligator hide and my normally brown hair sun-bleached to a golden hue. Kevin's hair was almost white. His usually fair skin was now the color of creamed coffee, and his shoulders were as freckled as a robin's egg. Neither of us had paid for a haircut since May. We looked like two boys from the movie *Lord of the Flies.*

There on Sunshine Lane, we both walked with our hands in our pockets, listening to traffic pass on Gulf Boulevard. Neither of us had mentioned our sex a single time that day, and I began to suspect that the taboos we'd shattered the previous night were something we would never discuss outside of my bedroom.

Maybe, I thought, *guys never talk about that sort of thing. The sex just happens, but it's not discussed.*

That was when Kevin asked me a question that seemed to come out of nowhere, something having nothing to do with sex. He said, "Has your mom told you what's wrong with *my* mom?"

I shook my head.

"It's what they call cervical cancer," he said, then pointed to his groin area. "It's in her private parts."

I crinkled my forehead. "Is it serious?"

Kevin nodded while he kept his gaze on the gravel before him. "She might make it, or she might not. The doctors don't know."

I licked my lips while I tried to process the information Kevin had just shared with me. *Mrs. Corrigan has cancer? Mrs. Corrigan might die?* The ideas seemed preposterous. She'd been such a large a part of my life in my early years, and she wasn't that old, maybe forty at most.

I cleared by throat. Then I said, "What happens if...?"

We kept on walking while Kevin talked.

"My dad couldn't take care of me on his own," Kevin said, "and I couldn't take care of him either. He'd go to a nursing home, I guess. I have an aunt in Boston—she's my mom's sister—and probably I'd go up there to live with her."

A weekly television series aired at that time, a cop show that took place in Boston. I'd watched a few episodes, and all I could remember was how *cold* things seemed up there. People wore overcoats and scarves, and the men wore wool fedora hats. Everyone spoke with those curious accents where they said "cah" instead of "car" and "bah" instead of "bar," and nobody, it seemed, had a yard in Boston. They lived in row houses with aluminum siding or in red brick apartment buildings with nary a shrub or architectural feature. I tried to imagine Kevin living in such a place, and I couldn't. He loved the outdoors; he was made for a warm-weather climate. Up in the frozen North, he'd probably wither like a corn stalk after harvest. And if Kevin moved to Boston, I'd probably never see him again, would I?

I tried to imagine myself in Kevin's position.

He's probably scared as hell, and who wouldn't be?

Chapter Five

A FULL MOON cast a silver rhombus onto my bedroom floor while I lay with my cheek resting on Kevin's chest. I listened to his heartbeat, to his soft breathing. Our sex had been a sweaty affair and my hair was damp. Kevin wrapped a few wet strands around his finger while he answered the question I'd just asked him.

"There's a guy in my neighborhood; he's a little older than me, a high school senior. Sometimes we do this when his folks aren't home. He taught me everything I know."

I rearranged my legs, but I kept my head on Kevin's chest. "Are you gay?" I asked.

He cleared his throat, then said, "I don't know, but maybe."

"Do you think *I'm* gay?"

Kevin chuckled.

"What's so funny?" I said.

Kevin rubbed his knuckle against the crown of my head. "You enjoy this; I can tell. It's like surfing: something you were meant to do."

Long after Kevin returned to his bed, I lay in mine, staring at the ceiling and thinking about what Kevin had told me: that our sex was something I was meant to do. I knew he was right, of course, but how would my peculiar needs affect my future?

TWO WEEKS HAD passed since Kevin's arrival, and already we'd fallen into a routine of sorts. Surfing, of course, consumed much of our daylight hours. Whenever we wore out our arm and shoulder muscles, we returned to my house, where we rinsed off in our outdoor shower room before changing into dry clothes.

Most nights, after doing the dinner dishes, we took a long walk on the deserted beach. The breeze would ruffle our hair while our bare feet squeaked in the wet sand. Phosphorous in the Gulf's water glowed whenever a wave broke on the shore. We talked about school or Kevin's

PAL baseball performances that spring. Or sometimes Kevin spoke of his father's declining health; it seemed the Colonel spent more time at the VA hospital than he did at home.

One particular night, we walked toward the Sea Castle Motel for an evening pool swim. We talked about the mischief we'd gotten into as kids in the Jungle, and I reminded Kevin of the dog turds he'd ignited on someone's doorstep.

"It was funny as hell," I said, "but you seem different now than you were back then. What's happened?"

Kevin grimaced while he rocked his head to one side. "Last year, I got into major trouble at school, once for fighting, another time for ice-picking a teacher's tire. My principal said I had to get counseling or he'd expel me, so now I see this lady. We talk about stuff: my family and all."

"Do you like it?"

Kevin shrugged. "It's all right, I guess. The lady thinks I suffer from what she calls 'low self-esteem.' It makes me angry, she says, and then I take it out on people around me. So I'm trying to work on that."

I nodded because what he'd just said didn't surprise me at all. "Do you have any friends?" I asked.

Kevin shook his head. "You know me; I've always been a loner. In fact, *you're* the only real friend I've ever had."

I pondered Kevin's last remark, then asked him a question that had dogged me for the past three years. "How come you never called or came to see me after you moved to Largo?"

Kevin took a few moments before he answered.

"I hated not seeing you, but what could I do about it? I figured we'd both be better off if we didn't stay in touch; it only would have made things worse if we had. But now that I'm here..."

"What?"

He stopped walking and so did I. Kevin worked his jaw from side to side while he looked at me. "I wish I could stay at your house forever," he said. "It's a real home, not like the place I live. There's no yelling and no sickness, plus spending time with you feels just right."

A sense of astonishment washed over me. Kevin, I then believed, had just told me in his own way that he loved me; that he always had, and that our separation had pained him just as much as it had me. Kevin's revelation was what I'd always hoped to hear from him but never expected, and now that he'd said it I was pretty sure a major barrier between us had fallen. I wanted to take Kevin into my arms, right there in the moonlight, so I could tell him I loved him too. And I might have done just that, but then Kevin pointed toward the Sea Castle Motel.

"Come on," he said. "That pool is waiting for us."

MY MOM TOOK Kevin and me to visit Mrs. Corrigan in the city's Catholic hospital, where many of the nurses were also nuns, and I even saw a Franciscan priest in his brown habit with a rope for a belt, and leather sandals. The hospital's hallways smelled of disinfectant, and I remember the whole place seeming very...quiet. People spoke in whispers.

Mrs. Corrigan looked pale and gaunt; her jowls sagged and her lips seemed thinner than ever before. But she smiled when she saw Kevin and me, and we both gave her a hug. She lay in a bed with her upper body raised and her lower body covered by a sheet and a thin blanket. She shared her room with another patient, a gray-haired woman with a cannula stuck in her nose who slept the entire time we were there. A water pitcher, a drinking glass, a Bible, and a rosary rested on Mrs. Corrigan's Formica-topped nightstand.

When Mrs. Corrigan talked, her voice sounded reedy. "The doctors say my operation was a success," she told my mom. "They removed the entire tumor—it wasn't that large—and it doesn't seem to have spread elsewhere."

My mom patted Mrs. Corrigan's wrist. "That's wonderful," she said.

"Is Kevin behaving?" his mom asked.

My mother nodded. "He's no trouble at all," she said. "In fact, he and Jesse are having a good time together." She looked at me and Kevin. "Isn't that right, boys?"

We both nodded, and then Kevin talked about the sandbar and all the surfing we'd done. "Jesse picked it up real quick," he said. I talked about the Velzy board I'd bought. Then we both talked about pool-hopping and walking the beach at night. In fact, we talked about *everything* we'd done so far, except for one very private and frequent activity.

"I'll be transferred to a nursing home four days from now," Kevin's mom told mine. "It's the same one where Frank is staying, so we can keep each other company. It'll be about eight weeks before I can finally come home and care for Frank again."

I looked at Mrs. Corrigan and wondered if she'd have the strength to do things like getting the Colonel out of bed or bathing the Colonel or getting him dressed. At the moment, she didn't look like she could do those things for herself, even. But then she'd just had major surgery, and maybe her present condition was only temporary. Maybe she'd rebound, but who knew?

SUMMER ROCKED ALONG. For a period of one week, we couldn't surf the sandbar because it was only above water during nighttime. So we took to fishing at the John's Pass Bridge, a structure only a ten-minute walk from my home. We bought live shrimp from a bait shop there, and we usually fished at night when the temperature was cooler. The place was a popular spot for anglers, and one guy or another always had a Coleman lantern burning so we could see what we were doing.

We caught a variety of fish at the bridge: red drum, flounder, pompano, red snapper, and speckled sea trout. We filleted our catches at a cleaning table with a fresh water faucet the City of Treasure Island provided, then brought the fillets home in a bucket. As mentioned before, my mom was a good cook, and she usually battered and fried our catches, which made for tasty meals when the fillets were combined with french fries, coleslaw, and tartar sauce.

"You boys are keeping the food bills down," Mom told us at the table one night. "It's a help and I appreciate it so much."

Kevin and I looked at each other and beamed. It felt good to know we were contributing something to our household that summer. Of course, we performed other chores as well: weeding our sand front yard and trimming the shrubs, washing my mom's convertible, and helping her bring groceries in from the car. We kept our beds made and my room neat. Kevin pitched right in—he never once complained—and it was nice having his help with things. We made a good team, I thought.

When I'd been younger, I always wondered what it might be like to have a brother, especially one older than me. Because my dad wasn't a part of my life, I'd never had a male influence other than Kevin, and he, of course, had never lived with us until now. But having him in our home day-to-day gave me a feel for the companionship an older brother might offer, and I liked it very much. Already I dreaded the day when Kevin would pack up his things and return to Largo.

How would I cope when he left me again?

Chapter Six

ON THE FOURTH of July, my mom, my sister, Kevin, and I attended a neighborhood potluck dinner party, where Kevin and I feasted on grilled hot dogs, baked beans, potato salad, corn on the-cob, and layer cake, all washed down with icy bottles of 7 Up. Once dinner was over and the sky had darkened, everyone headed to the beach to watch the city's fireworks display. The night was warm and breezy. Kevin and I wore our usual outfits: Bermuda shorts and T-shirts. Both of us were barefooted. By now the soles of our feet were as tough as leather; we almost never wore shoes of any kind.

I carried an old bedsheet for Kevin and me to sit on.

When we reached the shore, a sizeable crowd had gathered there. My mom and sister joined some of the folks we'd shared dinner with, but Kevin and I set out on our own. We found a sand dune blanketed with sea oats. The sea oats looked like a small wheat field, waving in the breeze. The dune had a sandy clearing in its center, sort of like a lagoon inside a coral atoll, and that was where we spread our sheet out. Once we sat on the sheet, no one could see us because we were surrounded by the sea oats, but we would still be able to see the fireworks when they ignited.

Earlier that day, Kevin and I had purchased a pack of L&M filtered cigarettes at a convenience store, and now we both lit up. The tobacco burned my lungs, but not unpleasantly, and then we both blew sheaths of smoke that the sea breeze quickly carried away. After we stubbed out our spent cigarettes, we lay on our sheet and gazed at the onyx sky; it was filled with twinkling stars. We spotted the Orion constellation and the Big Dipper. We studied the three-quarter moon and speculated on whether or not NASA would actually put a man up there before the end of the decade, as our late President Kennedy had pledged.

When the fireworks display began, we rose to sitting positions for a better view, and after a few rockets exploded, Kevin put his arm around my shoulders. His action took me by surprise; it was something he'd never done before. In fact he'd never shown any physical affection toward me outside of my bedroom, not beyond a hug or two. But now the weight of his arm and the warmth of his body made my heart thump.

It's almost like we're on a date.

In between fireworks, Kevin nuzzled my ear. I turned my face toward his, and then we kissed. Our tongues dueled while our lips smacked, and I grew so excited I thought I might piss in my shorts.

Next thing I knew, we lay on our sheet again, doing things gay boys do to each other when they're horny. Fireworks exploded; they bathed us in hues of green, red, blue, and gold. And then a white explosion lit up our dune like the glare from a lightning bolt. I felt as if we were performers in an exotic carnival act, only no one could see us inside our sea oat atoll. Our sex was intense and quick, and when it ended, we rested on our backs. Then we watched the fireworks go off, over and over.

Hiss.

Pop.

Ka-boom, and then *Ka-BOOM.*

FIVE WEEKS INTO Kevin's stay, on a Saturday afternoon, my mom drove us to the nursing home where Kevin's folks stayed. The home was a squatty cinder-block building with sparse landscaping and no trees to shade it from the relentless Florida sun. Heat shimmered off the asphalt pavement of the home's parking lot when we exited our car.

Inside, old folks in wheelchairs occupied the hallways. They stared into space as if they didn't know where they were. The whole place stank of urine and farts. Aides wearing scrubs and weary expressions lolled about a counter we passed. They seemed half-asleep.

The Corrigans shared a room with twin beds, a linoleum floor, and a single window offering a view of the nursing home's dumpster. The Colonel looked like he'd lost all the weight in his arms and legs; his limbs looked like toothpicks. Mrs. Corrigan didn't look too great herself. She was still haggard and she moved very slowly.

After we said hi to the Corrigans, my mom and I left Kevin with his folks so the three could chat privately. We found a sitting area with a vinyl sofa and a Formica coffee table littered with six-month-old copies of *Reader's Digest*. As soon as we sat, I asked my mom a question.

"What if Kevin's parents aren't able to care for him any longer?"

Mom looked at me and gathered her eyebrows. "I don't know," she said. "Why are you asking me?"

"I was thinking maybe Kevin could live with us, I mean...permanently."

Mom lowered her gaze; she rubbed her lips together.

I shifted my weight on the sofa while I pitched my idea. "It's not like he's a lot of trouble," I said. "In fact, he's a help. He and I could keep on sharing my room, and I'll bet his folks would give you money every month for his food and all."

Mom cocked her head to one side. "It's one thing for Kevin to stay with us for the summer, but once fall arrives, things might get complicated. How would he get to classes?"

"He could switch to our high school. We'd ride the bus together."

Mom shook her head. "You don't understand: the Corrigans are Catholic; they expect Kevin to attend a Catholic school. It's how things are with their religion. And besides, I don't think Kevin's parents will live in this nursing home much longer, maybe another five weeks or so, and then they'll go home. They'll want Kevin with them when they do."

"But what if they can't go home? What then?"

Mom gazed out a window where an ambulance idled in the parking lot.

She didn't answer my question.

ON A FRIDAY afternoon in mid-August, Kevin and I sat next to each other in the balcony of the State Theater in downtown St. Petersburg. We had ridden the bus from Treasure Island to see a spaghetti Western called *The Good, the Bad, and the Ugly*, starring Clint Eastwood. It was the kind of film appealing to boys our age, with Eastwood as antihero and plenty of gratuitous violence. Less than a dozen patrons viewed the film that day, so Kevin and I had the balcony to ourselves, and this allowed us to hold hands in the darkness.

We had reached a point in our relationship where we'd lost any hesitation about showing affection to each other whenever we had a modicum of privacy. We weren't just two boys fooling around anymore, at least not in my mind. We were bona fide lovers, an inseparable couple, but would that soon change?

Each time our telephone rang, I feared the caller might be Kevin's mom, informing us it was time for Kevin to leave my house. School would start in two weeks, for both me and Kevin, and something had to give. But so far, we'd heard nothing from the Corrigans.

Twice I'd again raised the subject of Kevin remaining with us, in talks with my mom, but both times she only said, "We'll have to wait and see."

So we waited, and as each day passed, my hopes grew that Kevin wasn't going anywhere, that he'd continue living under our roof and our personal relationship would live on. We had come so far, Kevin and I, since the end of our three-year separation. And now that we'd re-established the bond between us, how could life possibly pull us apart again?

Chapter Seven

THE NEWS CAME on August twenty-second, a rainy Monday.

Low tide that day was at six a.m. Kevin and I had hit the water at seven, as soon as daylight appeared. We paddled out to the sandbar while rain stippled the Gulf's surface and thunder rumbled in the distance. Then we surfed until our arms were noodles.

We returned to my home just after nine, where we rinsed ourselves off in our outdoor shower room, and then we changed into dry shorts. Inside the house, my sister sat at the dining table, using her portable sewing machine to stitch a skirt she planned to wear to school that fall.

When she saw us, she paused from her work and told Kevin, "Your mom wants you to call her at the nursing home."

Kevin looked at me and I looked at him. Then Kevin asked my sister, "What for?"

My sister only shrugged. "She didn't say."

Our phone sat on a desk in the living room, and after Kevin found the number for the nursing home's reception desk, he dialed while I slumped on my mom's easy chair. I kept my gaze fixed on Kevin while he asked the receptionist to transfer his call to his folks' room.

A few seconds passed, then Kevin said, "Hi, Mom, what's going on?"

Kevin stood there, listening to Mrs. Corrigan while twirling the phone's spirally cord around his finger, the way he sometimes did with strands of my hair after we'd had sex.

My sister ran her sewing machine, seemingly disinterested in Kevin's conversation, but I couldn't move a muscle. In fact, I could barely breathe. Kevin glanced at me for a moment, and when he did, I saw a vertical crease between his eyebrows that wasn't normally there.

Uh-oh.

A minute or so passed. Then Kevin said, "What time?" And a few seconds later, he told his mom, "Okay, I'll be ready."

By the time Kevin hung up, my blood had turned to ice. Already I knew, without Kevin even saying so, that he would leave us. I felt like I was sinking in quicksand. Kevin stood there at the desk, looking at me and working his jaw, and when he finally spoke, his voice sounded funny, like something was stuck in his throat.

"I'm moving back home today," he said. "My mom will be here at three."

My spirits sank like a stone cast into a pond. Three p.m.? With my sister in the house, that wouldn't even give us a chance to share a farewell screw. What could be worse? I cleared my throat and tried to keep my voice from trembling when I spoke.

"Can't you at least stay a few more days?" I asked.

Kevin shook his head. "I wish I could, but my folks are leaving the nursing home today; they want me back home with them. Plus I have to register for school. I need to buy uniforms and books: all that stuff. My mom says it can't wait; I have to leave this afternoon."

My eyes filled with tears when I rose from the easy chair. I didn't say another word; I just walked into my bedroom and closed the door behind me. Then I lay face down on my bed and wept while trying not to wail so my sister wouldn't hear my sobs. After a couple of minutes, Kevin opened the door and entered. After he closed the door and engaged the lock, he sat on the edge of my bed. He placed a hand on my shoulder.

"Jesse, you know I'd like to stay, but I can't."

I sniffled. "You could've at least asked for an extra day or two, but you didn't even do *that*."

Kevin ran his fingers through my hair while I sniffled some more. "You don't understand. My mom isn't back to normal—not yet anyway—and she's counting on me to help her with my dad. I need to be there."

"Okay," I said, "I get that, but when will I see you again?"

Kevin's voice sounded guarded when he answered. "It's hard to say. Even spending a weekend here is not going to happen anytime soon, not till my mom's stronger, and that could be a month or two; I just don't know."

"Then why don't I spend a weekend with you in Largo?"

Kevin hissed. "My home's not like yours. It wouldn't be the same as here. And my folks are always around; we'd have no chance to...you know."

After I flipped onto my back, I wiped snot from my upper lip with the back of my wrist, then interlaced my fingers behind my neck. But I still wouldn't look Kevin in the eye. My sorrow was quickly turning to anger.

"So," I said, "I guess this is it. And it'll be just like before, won't it? You'll never call or come to see me."

Kevin sat there, working his jaw.

"I'll try," he said, "but I'm not going to make any promises."

HOURS AFTER KEVIN departed in the Rambler wagon, with his surfboard sticking out of the wagon's rear window like a poked-out tongue, I sat amidst the sea oats in the dune where Kevin and I had watched Fourth of July fireworks, so many weeks before. I smoked one of the last L&M cigarettes from the pack we'd purchased that day. Visions of Kevin and me, doing all the things we'd enjoyed that summer, kept appearing in my mind's eye: surfing, pool-hopping, bridge-fishing, and of course, sex.

It's all over, I told myself.

I was pretty sure Kevin wouldn't call; he wasn't the type to do so, and he probably wouldn't visit either. He'd get busy with school and football and never have time for me.

That summer, I had fallen completely for Kevin; there was no doubt about that. But only after he left me did I realize just how much I loved him and how badly I craved his presence. There in the dune, I felt like someone had cut out my heart and fed it to a dog. My stomach ached and my head hurt.

I'd heard of people who killed themselves after breakups—they jumped off a bridge or whatever—and now I understood why those suicides happened. Now that Kevin was gone, I saw very little in the world that made me want to keep on going. Kevin had added a new dimension to my life that summer; he had helped me discover the real Jesse. He had validated my existence by making me feel desirable and special, but now he was back in Largo and I felt a lot like that teacher's tire Kevin had ice-picked at Bishop Keating High: deflated and useless.

Would my life ever feel meaningful again?

Chapter Eight

IN 1966, STUDENTS in Pinellas County attended three years of high school, and right after Labor Day, I started tenth grade at a school in south St. Petersburg, a prisonlike structure where two thousand students studied. Classrooms were crowded, as were the hallways and the cafeteria. In the boys' locker room, where we *had* to shower at the end of each PE class, muscular seniors snapped the tenth graders' butts with wet towels. They hurled insulting names at us like "punk" or "faggot" or "pussy."

I was still numb from losing Kevin and sort of sleepwalked through my days. I made no attempt to involve myself in campus activities. Who cared about service clubs or singing in the mixed chorus or joining the thespian society? I had already tasted the best life had to offer, courtesy of Kevin, and now my fellow students didn't interest me in the least.

Weekends, I surfed at the sandbar alone. I didn't enjoy the surfing all that much now that Kevin wasn't there to share the experience with me, but at least I was out there on the rolling water. I felt the sea breeze on my cheeks and the sun on my shoulders. Plus I could brood while I sat astride my Velzy and waited for a wave to ride.

I saw Kevin only once that fall, and it wasn't in person. One Saturday morning, I opened the sports page of the *St. Petersburg Times* to study our county's high school football scores, and there was a photo of Kevin in his uniform, racing across a goal line with a football under his arm and two opponents chasing him. Kevin, according to the game's summary, had intercepted a pass, then returned it forty yards for a touchdown. He was the first Bishop Keating safety to do so in many years, his coach said.

I studied the photograph for the longest time while rubbing my chin with a knuckle. I wondered whether Kevin had thought of me even once since the day of his departure from Treasure Island.

Why would he if he's getting this sort of attention from the world at large?

CHRISTMAS BREAK CAME. Despite my morose attitude toward life, I had worked hard at my fall studies and made honor roll the first two grading periods. My mom rewarded me with a Body Glove wetsuit as a Christmas gift so I could surf in the Gulf's chilly winter water whenever I chose to.

One weekday afternoon during the break, I had just showered after a two-hour surfing session. My dripping wetsuit hung on the clothesline in our courtyard. I had grown my hair out—it almost reached my shoulders now—and I decided to let my hair dry in the sunshine as well. The day was cool, but the sky was cloudless, the humidity low. I wore blue jeans, a hooded sweatshirt, and sneakers. I sat in our front yard on an Adirondack chair with my eyes closed; I savored the sun's rays on my face, then heard the rumble of a car's motor.

I opened my eyes to see Kevin behind the wheel of a shiny Ford Mustang fastback, a metallic blue number with two white racing stripes running from the tip of the hood all the way to the rear bumper. After parking in our driveway, Kevin leapt from the car like Robin exiting the Batmobile on TV. When Kevin did so, I let my gaze travel over his sleek frame, and like always, his beauty sent a shiver through my limbs. He wore corduroy Levi's, a V-neck sweater, and penny loafers that shone like mirrors. Sunlight reflected on his big teeth when he looked at me and smiled.

I didn't even get up from my chair. Despite Kevin's sexiness, I wasn't too happy about his surprise visit. After all, he had ignored me for nearly four months, so why should I make a big deal over the fact he'd finally decided to drop by? I raised a hand but didn't smile.

Then I said, "Nice car. Whose is it?"

Kevin walked up to me and mussed my damp hair. "Mine, stupid; it's a Christmas present from my folks."

I wasn't surprised. Kevin's parents always went overboard when buying him gifts—I think to make up for all the unhappiness in the Corrigan household—and I felt a tinge of jealousy as I studied the car's gleaming flank.

"I got my driver's license back in August," Kevin told me, "and now I have wheels. Want to take a spin?"

I couldn't say no, of course. The thought of cruising around town in Kevin's Mustang seemed irresistible. "Let me grab my wallet," I said.

Minutes later, we rolled down Gulf Boulevard with the radio blaring "Good Lovin'" by the Young Rascals and the wind fluttering our hair as it rushed through the car. Sunlight hammered on the Mustang's shiny hood while we passed hotels, gas stations, and restaurants. Traffic was light because the Northern tourists would not come to Florida until after the holidays ended.

"I saw your picture in the paper," I told Kevin.

He nodded. "Our team did great: eight wins and two losses. I won the defensive MVP award at the end-of-the-season banquet."

Of course, I thought.

When Kevin asked me about my high school and whether I liked it, I only shrugged. "It's nothing special," I said. "I don't get involved with anything there, other than attending class."

"Sounds boring," Kevin said.

I didn't reply to his observation; I only stared out the windshield while we idled at a stoplight.

"Done any surfing at the sandbar?" Kevin asked.

"Some," I said, then told him about the wetsuit I'd received for Christmas.

"I have one too," Kevin said. "Maybe sometime soon, I'll bring my board to your place. We can catch some rides."

After the light turned green, I stole a glance at Kevin while he accelerated, and it seemed to me that his facial features had grown even sharper since I'd last seen him, especially his cheekbones. Beneath his sweater, his shoulder and arm muscles bulged. If I hadn't known better, I would have fantasized about touching Kevin, but now I *did* know better. I wasn't going to let him hurt my feelings again, and I wouldn't pretend everything between us was rosy either.

"So," Kevin said, "besides surfing and going to school, what do you do with your time?"

"Not much," I said while I drummed my fingers on the passenger door's sill. "I watch TV, and I still have my yard-care business; it keeps me busy."

Kevin grunted. Then he asked, "Are you dating anyone?"

I looked at him and made a face. "Do you mean like...going out with a chick?"

He nodded like I'd stated the obvious, and in response, I blew air out my nose while I shook my head.

"What's wrong?" Kevin said.

"I'm *gay*. You know I don't like girls."

Kevin turned his gaze from me; he kneaded the Mustang's steering wheel as we left Treasure Island and crossed over a bridge. We entered St. Pete Beach where a new multistoried condominium towered over the Intracoastal Waterway. On the radio, an advertising jingle for a motorcycle dealership blared; it grated on my nerves so badly I switched off the radio entirely.

Kevin kept his gaze on the road before us while he cleared his throat. Then he said, "I thought maybe you'd changed. I figured since you're in high school now, you—"

"I *haven't* changed," I said, "but what do you care? You've got your new car and your football trophy, and I'm sure the girls are all after you, so why would you have any time for me?"

Kevin pursed his lips and shook his head. "You sound like a girl yourself; do you know that?"

Heat rose in my cheeks. I was so angry my vision blurred. "Oh, that's right," I said. "I'm like a girl and you're not. But remember something: you're the one who crawled into *my* bed the first time. You started things between us, or have you forgotten?"

Kevin's face turned as red as a ripe tomato while he kept his gaze straight ahead. Right away, I could tell I'd gotten under his skin. His usual cocky attitude was wavering, and so I kept on.

"What's the purpose of this visit today?" I said. "To show off your new car?"

Kevin's breath whistled in his nostrils when he looked at me. His chest rose and fell when he answered. "I came to see you 'cause I've missed you, and that's all. So why are you tossing shit in my face?"

I made a growling sound in my throat while I shook my head. "I haven't heard from you in four months. And why, because you're too busy to pick up the phone? Are you telling me you couldn't have spent at least one weekend with me, not in all that time?"

"You don't understand," Kevin said. "Friday nights there's football. Saturday nights we always have a dance in the gym at school. The girls from St. Mary's come over; it's a big deal."

"A big deal to whom?"

Kevin fluttered a hand. "To everyone."

I shook my head again. "So you'd rather spend time with girls from St. Mary's than me?"

Kevin pounded the Mustang's steering wheel with a fist. Then he yanked the wheel to his left. We screeched across two lanes of traffic and into the parking lot of a vacant restaurant. An oncoming car we'd nearly hit blared its horn in protest. When Kevin braked on the asphalt, his tires squealed. After he shifted to Park, he turned to me in his bucket seat. He got his face in mine, so close I smelled the corned beef sandwich he'd eaten for lunch.

"You're in high school now," he cried. "You have to grow up."

Now *I* was hollering. "I don't *want* to grow up; I want to be with you. I want you to spend the night with me so we can do the things we used to."

"But I *can't*. Don't you see that?"

I crossed my arms at my chest while I turned my gaze to the windshield. "Why not?" I said before returning my gaze to Kevin. "What's stopping you?"

Kevin lowered his gaze while he let out his breath. Then he looked into my face again. "If guys on the team knew I did that sort of thing, well...I'd probably get my teeth knocked out. You can't be gay and play football. You have to date girls; it's the way things work."

I scowled at Kevin. "You know what I think?"

"What?"

"I think you used me last summer, only 'cause it was convenient for you. I don't think you cared about me one bit, even though I cared for you a whole lot. And what an *idiot* I was for thinking we were actually boyfriends."

Kevin looked at me and blinked his eyes three or four times. "We *were* boyfriends, I guess. It's just we can't be any longer."

"Why, because you're too chickenshit to be who you really are?"

Kevin turned to face the windshield and slumped in his seat while he let out his breath again. We both sat there, listening to traffic pass on the boulevard.

Neither of us spoke for a minute or so until Kevin finally said, "What do you want from me, Jesse?"

"I already told you."

"And I just told you I can't."

"But you *could* if you really cared."

After Kevin drew a breath, he looked at his wristwatch. "I need to get back home; I'll drop you off on my way."

I flung the passenger door open. "Don't bother," I said while I left the car. "I'd rather walk."

Chapter Nine

MY TENTH-GRADE SCHOOL year ended before I knew it. My marks had been all As and Bs, and I was inducted into the National Honor Society on the last day of classes. But I still hadn't made a single friend or joined any sort of student organization. I must've seemed a sphinx to my classmates as I walked the campus hallways alone, keeping my gaze lowered and my facial expression stoic.

My family had moved, back in April, to a larger home only a block from our old house. The new one had a screened front porch, a full-size garage, a fireplace, and larger bedrooms. Now I enjoyed a queen-size bed, a better stereo system, and a bigger closet to store the clothes and shoes I'd bought with my yard-care earnings.

The day after classes ended, I canvassed our neighborhood, soliciting new customers. I owned a power mower, hedge clippers, and a power edger now, so I didn't have to use my customers' equipment any longer, which helped me get more business. After three days, my customer base had grown from four to twelve, and in the weeks ahead, I kept busy from eight in the morning till five in the afternoon, five days per week. I took weekends off to surf, fish, and sleep.

My workdays were brutal. By eleven a.m., the temperature hit ninety-two most every day, and the humidity was equally high. I drank water like a camel from garden hoses. I wore a broad-brimmed straw hat, a long-sleeved T-shirt, cut-off blue jeans, and work boots. By now, I was close to six feet tall, with long arms and legs and stringy muscles. I weighed 155 pounds.

Every weekday I came home exhausted, caked in a mixture of dirt and sweat, with grass clippings stuck to my calves and forearms. I was so filthy I'd wash up in our outdoor shower room before I even entered the house. But I didn't care. The work kept me busy and the money rolled in. Even after buying gas for the mower and edger, I still cleared about seventy dollars a week, a lot of money for a fifteen-year-old kid to earn at the time.

My sister and her best friend had both taken jobs as junior counselors at a summer camp for girls in the mountains of western North Carolina; Lisa wouldn't return to Florida until mid-August. My mom, of course, kept busy with her full-time job at a bank, and with her volunteer work at the St. Petersburg children's hospital. Outside of sharing our evening meal, Mom and I saw little of each other.

I suppose a lot of boys my age would have felt lonely in my situation, but I honestly never did. While I pushed my mower or edged someone's sidewalk, I daydreamed about moving to California or maybe Hawaii one day, where I could test my surfing skills on waves larger than the sandbar's. And often, of course, I thought about Kevin; I recalled the previous summer when we'd shared so many days and nights together.

Whenever I thought of my summer with Kevin, it occurred to me that I had been awfully needy when he moved in with us. When Kevin placed my hand between his legs that night at the drive-in theater, he set loose a beast within me, a sexual animal with a healthy appetite. Back then, I didn't know how to control the beast, and when Kevin left for Largo, the beast drove me insane with a sense of loss. For months, I craved Kevin's presence so badly my belly ached.

Now, nearly a year after Kevin's departure, I'd grown wiser. I knew better than to open my heart to Kevin or anyone else, not without being careful. I kept to myself, and I assuaged the beast as best I could with a tube of jelly and my right hand.

One of my customers had a son, a slender guy about my age with a swish in his gait, a turned-up nose, pale skin, and a mop of auburn hair falling across his green eyes. More than once, I'd heard neighborhood people make derisive comments about how feminine he looked. Often while I mowed his parents' lawn, he sat on their shaded back door stoop, smoking a cigarette and watching me work. One afternoon, while I sweated under a broiling sun, he offered me a cold bottle of Sprite and a Marlboro. We sat on his door stoop. He told me his name was Spencer, and after we shook hands, he looked right and left. Then he placed his hand on my thigh.

"My folks work in Tampa; they won't be back for hours," he said while his gaze drilled into mine. Then he jerked his head toward his back door. "Let's have some fun in my bedroom."

I felt shocked by his boldness and tempted by his offer. I hadn't touched another guy since my last session with Kevin the previous summer, and the thought of touching Spencer had my pulse galloping. But then I thought, *What will this lead to?* I didn't even *know* Spencer. Could I really trust him? What if he told a neighbor that we'd fooled around? Or what if I fell in love with him like I'd fallen for Kevin? What then? Did I really want my feelings hurt a second time?

I looked down at Spencer's hand for a long moment. After I seized his wrist and lifted it from my leg, I looked into his eyes and shook my head. Then I swung my gaze to the yard while I took a drag off my Marlboro.

"Are you sure?" Spencer asked me.

"Yeah," I said, "I'm sure."

ON A THURSDAY afternoon in early August, our house shook every time another thunderclap sounded. Squall lines blew over Treasure Island from the Gulf, one after another. Rain drummed the roof and lightning flashed. Already, puddles had collected in our front yard and the gutters on the street carried a steady stream of water toward a storm-sewer opening on the corner.

I had come home for lunch, just before the storms began, and after rain started falling, I phoned my afternoon customers to tell them I couldn't work on their yards when they were wet. I'd have to come on Saturday, I told them, after things dried out. I was rinsing my lunch dishes in the kitchen sink when I heard a sound in our driveway, one I instantly recognized: the rumble of a Ford Mustang's muffler.

Right away, my stomach clenched.

What's he *doing here?*

When I answered Kevin's knock, he stood on our doorstep with a raindrop hanging off the tip of his nose. His hair was plastered to his skull and his clothing was soaked.

"Can I come in?" he asked in a croaky voice.

"Why?" I said. "What for?"

"I need to talk to you."

After I motioned him inside, he asked for a towel and a change of clothes. In my room, he peeled off his wet clothing, even his briefs, and right away, my mouth grew sticky at the sight of his naked flesh. His muscles rippled; he looked like a Greek statue I'd once seen in a *National Geographic* magazine.

While he toweled himself, I asked him, "How come you're all wet?"

"I went to your old house; I kept banging on the front door then the back one, until a neighbor with an umbrella came over; she said you'd moved here. By that point, I was drenched."

I nodded while he dried his hair, and when he'd finished doing that, he stepped into a clean pair of briefs I'd given him. Then he sat on the edge of my bed. His gaze traveled around the room before he returned it to me.

"You're working today?" he asked.

"I *was*, but with all the rain, I had to quit."

Kevin lowered his gaze. He cleared his throat a time or two and looked into my face. "I came to tell you something."

"What?"

"My dad died yesterday, at the VA hospital. He had a stroke caused by a blood clot; it traveled to his brain."

I winced while I sat on a bedside chair that creaked under my weight. I recalled the last time I'd seen the Colonel in the nursing home where he and Kevin's mom had lived for a spell, and I recalled how unhealthy he looked. Despite the fact he'd been a cantankerous guy, he had always been kind to me, and now I felt a twinge of sadness when I realized I'd never see him again. I wouldn't hear his barking at Kevin, nor would I smell the smoke from his Hav-A-Tampa cigars.

"I'm sorry," I said. "I know he was tough to live with, but still...he was your dad."

Kevin lowered his gaze and nodded.

"How's your mom doing?" I asked.

"She's sad, of course—they were married twenty-two years—but in a way, it's a blessing he died. These past few years, Mom spent half her life toting him back and forth to the VA. And it got to where he couldn't go anywhere or do anything. He watched TV and that was about it."

I asked about the funeral.

"It'll be next week—on Saturday, I think. Can you make it?"

I nodded.

Kevin made no attempt to put on the clothes I'd loaned him. He just sat there in my briefs while staring at the floor and looking like someone had knocked the wind out of him on the playing field.

"Are *you* okay?" I asked.

He looked at me and shook his head while his eyes glistened. His voice had a shake to it when he answered. "It's hard, you know, losing someone you've known all your life; it's very hard. And there's no one I can talk to about it but you."

Ah-h-h, shit.

My knees crackled when I rose from my chair. I sat down on the bed next to Kevin and put my arm across his shoulders. Right away, he hung his head and wept. His body shook and tears fell onto his sinewy thighs. Outside, another thunderclap sounded. Rain drummed the roof and wind gusts rattled the windows.

I waited a few minutes to speak, until Kevin's sobs ceased. "It'll be okay," I told him while he wiped away tears with a wrist and sniffled.

"I don't know," he said. "Now it's just Mom and me, and she's not all that well either. What if something happens to *her?* What then?"

I considered telling Kevin that maybe he could live with us, but I wasn't all that crazy about the idea, not after all I'd gone through since the last time he stayed at our house. I was still very angry and hurt about the way he'd ignored me after moving back to Largo. But it was hard to be mad at Kevin when he was so distraught.

"Your mom will be fine," I said. "She'll always be there for you."

He looked at me with his red and swollen eyes. "What about you?" he said.

"What do you mean?"

"Will *you* still be here for me?"

I didn't know what to say. In a sense, I thought it was pretty damned nervy of Kevin to ask me a question like that, considering the way he'd treated me. But then I thought of him standing in the rain at our old house, banging on the doors while the storm soaked him, and remembered something Kevin had once told me:

"You're the only real friend I've ever had."

I knew it was true. He had no one else to turn to but me at such a difficult moment, and I'd be a total shit if I didn't honor our friendship, as strained as it was by Kevin's selfish neglect of my needs.

So I squeezed his shoulders with my arm and said, "Of *course* I'll always be here for you. We've been friends forever; why would that change?"

Kevin sniffled. Then he rubbed the tip of his nose with a knuckle. "The last time I saw you, when we took that ride in my car, I thought I might not ever see you again. You were mad at me, and I guess you had a right to be."

I nodded. "I don't understand why you don't stay in touch. If we're going to be friends, then you have to call me; you have to come see me once in a while. And there's one more thing."

"What?"

I nuzzled Kevin's ear and kissed his cheek. "You can't be afraid to touch me like you used to; it's important. And you don't have to worry, I won't tell anyone."

He nodded. Then he looked into the hallway. "Where's your sister right now?"

I explained.

"And your mom?"

"She's at work; she won't be home till five thirty."

Kevin reached between my legs; he gave me a squeeze. Then he looked at me and raised his eyebrows. "Do you want to touch me right now?"

My pulse raced, but should I do this? Would Kevin only hurt me again? "I'm dirty and smelly from work," I said. "Maybe another—"

Kevin squeezed my crotch a second time. "Take a shower; I can wait."

Aye-yi-yi, I thought. *Go on: do it.*

By the time I returned to my bedroom, the briefs I'd loaned Kevin rested on the floor. He lay on my bed with his head in the pillows and an elbow bent behind his head. I lay down beside him and trembled so hard the bedsprings squeaked.

It's really happening, I told myself when I laid a hand on Kevin's chest. *This is what I've wanted ever since he left for Largo.* Our sex was aggressive and sweaty, and in the middle of it all, while Kevin worked his hips, he blurted out something I will never forget.

"Jesus Christ, I've never felt so good in my life."

I found it a bit odd that Kevin would say such a thing only a day after his dad's death, but maybe having sex with me was just the sort of emotional release Kevin needed at the moment. When it was over and we lay in each other's arms, all I could think was, *I want to do this every day.* And then I wondered, *When will I see him again?*

Just before Kevin departed, and after we placed his wet clothing in a grocery sack to take with him, I made Kevin promise me two things: he would call me every Thursday night at eight so we could talk, and at least once a month, even during football season, he would spend a Saturday night with me.

Whether or not Kevin intended to *keep* those promises, I wasn't sure, but at least he'd *said* he would.

An hour after Kevin left the house, I still smelled his piney scent on my skin. I lay on my sticky sheets, listening to rain drip from our roof's eaves. The air was damp and cool, and the acrid scent of the lubricant we'd used was strong in the room. Traffic on Gulf Boulevard hissed and mumbled while I ran scenes of my sex with Kevin through my head. I heard our lips smack, felt Kevin caress my tender flesh with his tongue. I recalled the power of his sleek body as he thrust inside me.

In a sense, it was our first time all over again because we had changed so much over the past year. We were different people now, both physically and mentally. We were larger and stronger, and maybe a little smarter too.

While I lay in my bed, I marveled at all that had happened that afternoon. Before Kevin fell apart and wept in my room, I honestly thought I would never touch him again. But now it seemed we had ignited something new between us, something more intense and mature than what we'd shared the previous summer. By shedding tears in my presence, Kevin had allowed me to witness his vulnerability, and I knew he'd only done so because he trusted me not to think less of him for crying.

Was it possible I'd become Kevin's equal now instead of his protégé? By chewing him out that day in his car, then by insisting he do a better job of maintaining our friendship, I'd let Kevin know he couldn't take me for granted, nor would I tolerate his neglect. Maybe now he understood that he'd have to work for my friendship in order to keep it.

The question was, would he?

Chapter Ten

THE THURSDAY FOLLOWING Kevin's visit, I sat on the easy chair in our living room. The time was close to eight p.m. and I stared at the telephone on our desk, waiting for Kevin's call. Minutes ticked by while I chewed my lips and bounced my heels. I turned the pages of a *Life* magazine, but I wasn't even paying attention to the photos or the text.

My sister had returned from North Carolina two days before, and now she practiced her clarinet in her bedroom. Although her door was closed, I could still hear the screeching of the instrument and it only added to the tension I felt inside me. My mom was visiting a friend down the street so I had the living room to myself. Rising, I paced back and forth between the front door and the fireplace, while running my fingers through my hair. Why wasn't Kevin calling me? Had he already forgotten his promises?

By eight thirty, I was going nuts. I considered calling Kevin myself, but decided against it. Phoning Kevin would only make me seem too needy; it would undermine whatever progress I thought I'd made the week before when we had reached our agreement. Or did we even *have* an agreement?

Finally, by eight forty, I knew Kevin wasn't going to call. Feeling frustrated and angry, I swiped two cigarettes from my mom's pack of Viceroys, then headed for the beach. The night was warm and breezy and a close-to-full moon hung in the western sky; it cast a silver ribbon onto the Gulf's placid surface. I was barefooted, and I trod the water's edge, feeling wet sand ooze between my toes. Every time I took a puff off my cigarette, the ash glowed a bright orange.

I seethed at the way Kevin had casually ignored our deal on the first opportunity he'd had to honor it. I felt foolish and put down and oh so dumb for believing Kevin and I had something serious going on between us when clearly we didn't. When I last saw Kevin, he'd only told me whatever I wanted to hear without really meaning what he said. I shook my head in disgust, then remembered that the Colonel's funeral was two days off. My mom and I had made plans to attend, but maybe out of revenge, I *wouldn't* go. I could show Kevin that I could ignore his needs just like he had ignored mine.

But no, I couldn't disrespect the Colonel and Mrs. Corrigan by not attending the funeral, no matter how angry I was with Kevin. I'd have to put aside my hurt feelings and do the right thing.

But I'll sure give Kevin an earful if I get the chance.

THE FUNERAL WAS held in a small chapel next to the main St. Jude sanctuary, where an organist played somber music and two wizened ushers handed out programs. Mrs. Corrigan and Kevin greeted a short line of mourners in the chapel's foyer. Most were older folks; many wore VFW garrison caps. Kevin wore a navy-blue blazer, charcoal dress slacks, and his penny loafers, and despite the fact I was furious with him, I had to admit he looked very handsome in his outfit.

When we reached Kevin and Mrs. Corrigan, Kevin gave my mom a hug, but when he tried to hug me, I only stuck out my hand. I didn't smile or say hi either. Kevin looked at my hand and frowned, but then we shook and I moved on to Mrs. Corrigan, who looked a bit shell-shocked. I gave her a hug and told her I was sorry about the Colonel.

"Thanks for coming," she told me. "It means so much to Kevin that you're here."

And I thought to myself, *I don't really think that's true.*

The service was conducted by a young priest wearing vestments. Thankfully he spoke in English instead of Latin. He talked about the Colonel's war service and his wounds and how bravely he'd handled his post-war disability. He described the Colonel as a "loving husband and father," and I found myself wondering whether the priest had ever actually *known* the Colonel. Had he heard some of the abusive epithets the Colonel often hurled at Kevin?

At the end of the service, which was mercifully short, the priest announced that refreshments would be served in the church's social hall, adjacent to the chapel. I didn't want to attend, but my mom insisted we go. It would be rude not to, she said.

In the social hall, I barely had time to pour myself a cup of punch before Kevin sidled up to me and threw an arm around my shoulders. "Are you busy tonight?" he asked. "I thought I'd sleep at your place if it's okay with you and your mom."

My heart skipped a beat when he made his request. Of *course* I wanted Kevin to spend the night; I wanted it more than anything in the world. But I couldn't just say yes without bringing up his failure to phone me.

I looked left and right to see if anyone could overhear me. Then I said, "What happened to the agreement we made last week? I waited forty minutes for you to call on Thursday, but you never did."

After Kevin withdrew his arm from my shoulders, he stuffed his hands in his pants pockets while he studied the tops of his penny loafers. "Sorry," he said, then looked up. "I kind of forgot."

"You forgot? A deal is a deal, and I expect you to keep your end up."

"Jeez," Kevin said, shaking his head. "It was just a phone call."

"Yeah, but it was an *important* one."

Kevin let out his breath. "Let's not argue, okay? I said I was sorry and I meant it. Now should I come over tonight or not?"

I chewed my lips for a moment.

Go on, jackoff, don't be stupid.

"Of course," I said. "Do you want to have dinner with us?"

Chapter Eleven

HIGH SCHOOL FOOTBALL season commenced right after Labor Day, and even though my mom had zero interest in football, I somehow coaxed her into taking me to Bishop Keating's first home game, an evening contest against a Catholic high school from Tampa. Nearly eight hundred people filled the bleachers on the Keating side of the field, on a warm and humid night. A priest said a prayer before the game commenced, and everyone bowed their heads until the priest was finished.

Then everyone said out loud, "Holy Mary, mother of God, pray for us sinners," which I thought was an odd way to start a football game.

Kevin, of course, looked magnificent in his black jersey and football pants and his bright yellow helmet that reflected the glow of the field lights. His jersey number was thirty-five. Ten minutes into the game, he intercepted a long pass, then ran it back about twenty yards before an opponent pushed him out of bounds. The Keating faithful roared their approval, and the Keating head coach rewarded Kevin with a pat on the ass when Kevin came to the sideline.

Keating won the game by a score of 28-0, and by the end of the contest, I understood why Kevin had won his trophy the previous season. The receivers Kevin defended almost never caught a ball. Kevin consistently batted passes down; he covered the receivers like a blanket. He even made another interception during the second half, ending the opposing team's only real chance to score a touchdown.

When the Keating team filed toward their locker room, I hollered at Kevin from the railing at the bottom of the stands, and when he saw it was me, he waved. Then he gave me a one-hundred-watt smile that made me feel like the luckiest guy in the world.

Okay, Kevin hadn't once called me on a Thursday since the funeral, and I quickly came to realize he probably never would. "I'm not a phone person," he told me when I finally called *him*. "I shouldn't have made that promise, but I'm sticking to the other one for certain."

So far he had. In fact, he'd already spent the night with me *twice* after his stay the night of the funeral, and all three times, he'd been just as lusty as I. My sheets were always a mess the morning after Kevin slept over, and I sometimes wondered if Mom knew exactly what went on in my room when Kevin visited.

One Sunday morning, I woke to find Kevin's cheek resting on my shoulder, one of his legs crossed over one of mine, and his arm draped across my chest. I buried my nose in his wavy hair to inhale its grassy scent. I stroked his forearm with a fingertip, feeling the fine hairs that grew there while I listened to him breathe.

God, I'm lucky, I told myself.

Kevin's visits to Treasure Island weren't just satisfying my sex drive— they also helped with my self-confidence. Once again, I felt desirable and worthy like I had that summer Kevin lived with us. I took better care of my appearance, walked with a more purposeful stride. I even joined the Junior Civitans at school, a boys' service club with fifty or so members, most of them kids from beach communities who surfed or skateboarded in their free time.

One Saturday morning, a dozen Junior Civitan members, myself included, helped paint a clubhouse owned by the Holiday Isles Civitan Club, an adult organization that sponsored us. The clubhouse was located in Redington Beach, about ten miles north of Treasure Island, and right on the sandy shore. The building was cinder block with wood trim, so it was easy to paint with rollers and brushes. The day was warm and most of us shed our shirts. When lunchtime came, the adults treated us to a cookout, and then my club's members took a swim in the Gulf.

One Junior Civitan member, a tall and broad-shouldered boy named Lane Davis, struck up a conversation with me while we swam. We shared two classes at school, and he was also in the National Honor Society, so we had a few things in common. Lane told me he lived on Causeway Isles, between Treasure Island and St. Petersburg. I told him where I lived, and when I spoke of the sandbar I surfed at, his gray eyes sparkled.

"I have a board," he said. "Invite me over sometime."

We spent the rest of the afternoon working side by side with paint rollers, and while we worked, we talked. Lane's voice had a rasp to it. He was sixteen; he had a driver's license and a car, a VW Beetle with dented fenders, chalky paint, and a surfboard rack attached to the roof. His sandy-colored hair was as straight as straw; it grew to his shoulders, which were speckled with the light blue paint we applied to the clubhouse walls. His dad was a pharmacist, his mom an elementary school teacher, and he planned to attend the University of Florida after graduating from high school.

I felt a pang of envy as Lane spoke of such things. I hadn't seen my dad since I was six; I didn't even know where he lived or what his job was. My mom was a junior bank officer, and as for college, I hadn't even thought about going. Wasn't a university education costly?

At the end of the day, Lane offered me a ride home. "It's right on my way," he said, and then we tooled down Gulf Boulevard in his VW with the muffler growling and the gears grinding as Lane worked the stick shift. Warm wind rushed through the car; it ruffled our hair while we jabbered away, and it occurred to me as we crossed the John's Pass Bridge that I might have found a new friend in Lane, my first in a very long time.

Before I knew it, Lane was braking at the curb before my house, and when I turned to thank him for the ride, he extended his hand. We looked into each other's eyes while we shook, and I felt the warmth of Lane's palm against mine.

"I'll see you in class on Monday," Lane said, then drove away while I stood on the sidewalk, thinking about the hours we'd shared that day. I knew it never would have happened if I hadn't joined the Junior Civitans, and I never would have joined the club were it not for my newfound confidence that stemmed from my rekindled relationship with Kevin.

While I watched Lane's car disappear around the corner, my lips moved as I spoke to Kevin. "Thank you," I whispered, "for making this day happen."

SEPTEMBER GAVE WAY to October, and then summer's heat finally began to ebb. I didn't always gulp water from my customers' garden hoses when I mowed their lawns. Because of school, I had cut back to six lawns per week. I mowed three on Saturdays and the other three on weekdays after school. That still netted me thirty dollars each week, and by now, I had saved over five hundred dollars.

My birthday fell on October twelfth, a Thursday, and with my mom's permission, I skipped my morning classes at school. She took the morning off from work so she could drive me to the DMV, where I took my practical exam for a driver's license. I was nervous as hell, of course, but I'd practiced with Mom's car for six months after obtaining a learner's permit, and right after I flawlessly parallel parked between two orange cones in the DMV parking lot, I left with my shiny new license. It featured an unflattering headshot of me that made me look like I had something sizeable stuck up my butt.

My next goal, of course, was to buy a car. For weeks, I'd scanned classified ads in the *St. Petersburg Times*, looking at listings for used vehicles. There were hundreds, and I felt confused by all the terminology the ads used like "horsepower" and "warranty" and "four-on-the-floor." At school, I visited our auto-mechanics instructor, a slick bald guy with horn-rimmed glasses and a pen caddy in his shirt pocket. I talked with him about what sort of car I ought to purchase and how much I should pay for it.

"Don't buy a sports car or anything flashy," he told me. "You need basic transportation, something that doesn't burn a lot of gasoline and won't cost much to repair. You can buy something decent for about three hundred dollars if you look hard enough."

I got lucky: one of my customers on Treasure Island, an octogenarian whose eyesight was failing, decided to sell her 1963 Dodge Dart. She had kept the car garaged and its odometer read only 35,228 miles. When she told me she planned to sell the Dart, I offered her three hundred dollars. The car was probably worth more than that, but she liked me and so she gave me a break: we settled on $350. I paid her in cash, and then we visited her bank where she signed the title over to me in the presence of a Notary Public.

Now *I* had wheels.

Okay, maybe it was an "old-lady car," as Kevin tagged it the first time he saw it, but the Dart's vinyl upholstery was in great shape, the body had no rust on it and everything mechanical worked: the radio, the power steering, and even the clock. The Dart's slant-six engine didn't burn much gas either. The first Sunday after I bought the car, I washed it in our driveway, then applied a coat of Simonize wax to its metallic blue-gray paint. When I was done, the Dart looked like it belonged on a dealer's showroom floor.

The following morning, I drove my car to school, feeling very much the adult. I even gave Lane Davis a ride, since he lived right on my way. The two of us rolled down First Avenue South in St. Petersburg while the radio played a Buffalo Springfield song titled "For What It's Worth."

Lane had already visited my home once on a Sunday, with his Chuck Dent surfboard strapped to the roof rack on his VW. We took our boards to the beach, then paddled to the sandbar to ride waves. We had the bar to ourselves. The waves came at us in sets of three, and we surfed till both of us felt exhausted. Lane was a good surfer, almost as skilled as Kevin. He moved fluidly on his board and he knew how to get the most out of any wave he caught. When we were done, we sat on the sandbar's shore, staring at the Gulf's rolling surface and gabbing away.

I'd never had a friend like Lane before. He was bright and self-assured but wasn't the least bit arrogant. His interests were varied. He liked following the national and state political scenes; he was a staunch Democrat, and he opposed our country's involvement in the Vietnam War. He attended a Unitarian church with his parents every Sunday morning, and he volunteered at the church's soup kitchen on Wednesday evenings.

When I asked Lane what he planned to study at the university, he said he wasn't sure yet. "Maybe journalism or law," he said. "Or I might go for a teaching degree; I just don't know."

"Isn't the university expensive?" I asked.

Lane shrugged. "Not really. I mean, if you live in a dorm and eat on the meal plan you can get by on two thousand bucks per school year, and a student loan will cover four years of that, no problem."

I crinkled my forehead. "What's a student loan?"

"A bank or a credit union lends you the money for school. Your parents have to cosign. The government guarantees repayment of the loan, so there's really no risk for the lender. Once you graduate, you have ten years to pay off your loan."

I nodded while I pondered what Lane had just told me. Since my mom *worked* at a bank, maybe she could help me get a student loan through her employer. Who knew?

Now, as I pulled the Dart into our school's student parking lot, Lane asked me if I had plans for the upcoming Sunday.

I shook my head.

"My folks have a powerboat we keep at our dock. Would you like to water-ski with us?"

I, of course, had never been on a boat in my life. "I don't know how to ski," I told Lane.

He swatted the air with his hand. "It's not hard; I can teach you in no time."

I tried to imagine myself gliding behind a gleaming boat with a powerful outboard engine, as I'd seen other people do. Could I do it too, or would I make a fool out of myself in front of Lane and his folks?

Go ahead; don't be a chickenshit.

"All right," I said. "What time should I be there?"

THREE DAYS LATER, at exactly eight p.m., our desk phone rang, and I nearly fell over backward when I heard Kevin's voice on the line.

"Jesse?"

"Yeah, it's me. I can't believe you actually called for once, and right on time."

"Well I did, so now you owe me."

I grunted. "Exactly *what* do I owe you?"

Kevin snickered. "You'll see," he said. "Listen, my team has a bye this week, so—"

"A what?"

Kevin hissed. "A *bye*, dummy; it means we don't play a game on Friday, so I'm free the whole weekend. I thought I'd stay with you Friday and Saturday nights; how about it?"

My spirits soared. Not only had Kevin phoned per our agreement, but we would actually spend an entire weekend together. What could be better?

"Sounds great," I said. "I'll have three yards to mow on Saturday, but if you'll help me, we can knock them out real quick in the morning. Low tide's around two p.m. on Friday; then it's a half hour later on Saturday, so we'll get some surfing in for sure."

"Perfect," Kevin said.

FRIDAY AFTERNOON, ON my way home from school, I made a stop at the Treasure Island Rexall pharmacy to purchase a fresh tube of jelly. When I stepped to the cash register, I found Spencer, my customers' auburn-haired son, standing behind the counter. He wore a dark blue smock with the Rexall logo on the chest.

"Hey, Jesse," he said, and then his gaze traveled to the jelly tube I'd placed on the counter.

"Hi, Spencer; how are you?"

He didn't respond; he only checked the tube's price label and rang up the sale. After he placed the tube in a paper sack, he gazed right and left. Then he looked at me and winked. "Planning on a fun weekend?"

I felt heat in my cheeks while I lowered my gaze. I picked up the sack with the jelly tube inside it. Then I looked at Spencer and made a little smile. "Actually I am," I said. "How about you?"

He shrugged. "Not really, but that could change. Why don't you pay me a visit tomorrow? Say...right around noon?"

"Thanks," I said, "but I have plans. I'll see you around."

When I got home, Kevin's car sat on our driveway and his surfboard leaned against an outside wall of our garage. Inside the house, I found Kevin and my sister fast-dancing to the Supremes' song "Love is Here and Now You're Gone." My sister was a decent dancer, but Kevin was enthralling to watch. He moved like a seductive animal in his Keating uniform. His hips twitched and his butt shook while his arms moved to the beat of the music. Both he and my sister were laughing like idiots.

"What's so funny?" I hollered over the music.

After my sister turned off the radio, she looked at me and rubbed the tip of her nose. "Kevin's been telling me stories about the girls from St. Mary's. I guess they're not as pure as they're made out to be."

I looked at Kevin and raised an eyebrow. "How so?"

My sister answered before Kevin could. "You know those Saturday night dances at Bishop Keating? It seems like the *real* action happens in the parking lot, not inside the gym."

I rolled my eyes and asked Kevin if he wanted to surf the sandbar.

"Let's do it," he said, and moments later, we changed into surfing trunks in my bedroom. Afternoon sunlight entered through the western windows; the light reflected in Kevin's pubic hair. His nakedness got me so excited I would have grabbed him and pushed him onto the bed had my sister not been there to overhear us.

A light sea breeze tickled our cheeks as we carried our boards to the shore, where we waxed the boards' decks before wading into the warm Gulf water. Already I heard waves break at the bar. While we paddled out, side by side, I asked Kevin a question.

"Are you part of the parking lot action at those dances?"

Kevin glanced at me for only a moment before returning his gaze to the western horizon. "Once in a while, yeah. It's all part of going to the dance."

"So, you bring girls to your car and then you do things with them?"

"Of course; it's what they want."

I made a face like I'd just sucked on a lemon. "Is that what *you* want?"

He glanced at me again, then looked away. "Look," he said, "I'm on the football team; it's expected. If I didn't do it, people might think there was something wrong with me."

"You mean they might think you were gay?"

Kevin stopped paddling. He sat up straight and put his hands on his hips. I stopped paddling too, and then the two of us faced each other; we floated in the placid water while salty droplets glistened on our shoulders.

Kevin said, "That stuff in the parking lot doesn't mean anything to me, so don't be jealous. I'm spending this weekend with you because I want to."

"But—"

Kevin held up a hand. "Forget the St. Mary's girls, will you?"

He's right, I told myself. *This weekend's all about you and Kevin, so don't spoil it.*

"Okay," I said. "I'll do that."

THAT WEEKEND, KEVIN spent with me seemed more like a dream than reality, at least until the very end of his visit. October's weather was still warm, but far less humid, and a breeze always blew to keep us comfortable. I didn't even mind tending my customers' lawns because I wasn't sweating so much, plus Kevin helped me by edging driveways and trimming shrubs. Surf at the sandbar was larger than normal, almost shoulder height, and thus more challenging and fun.

Friday night, we fished at the John's Pass Bridge, where Kevin caught two red drum and I a Nassau grouper. We brought the fillets home in a bucket, and on Saturday night, my mom prepared a tasty fish dinner. After we washed the dishes, Kevin and I pool-hopped at three motels. Then we walked back to my house in our damp surfing baggies, smelling of chlorine. We strolled along the deserted shore, holding hands, and I don't think I'd ever felt so contented with my life.

That weekend, Kevin seemed more relaxed as well. Conversation flowed freely between us, and several times, he touched me affectionately. He ruffled my hair or stroked my forearm, or he patted my ass when others weren't around. He even put his arm around my shoulders while we watched TV by ourselves on the living room sofa.

Of course, the best parts of that weekend were our sex sessions in my bedroom. The cool night air flowing through the windows seemed to energize us. All that slurping and smacking, along with the squishy sound of the jelly we used, drove me crazy with lust.

When I woke Sunday morning, Kevin lay on his side with his back to me. I brought my hips to his buttocks and my chest to his shoulder blades. Then I wrapped my arm around Kevin's waist while I buried the tip of my nose in his wavy hair. The air was still and cool. I listened to waves smack the shore to the west, then told myself, *I wish this weekend would never end.*

But of course it did end, and not well.

When we rose, my mom and sister had already gone to church, so we had the house to ourselves. We could hang out naked. While we munched on bowls of cornflakes at the dining table, Kevin asked me when low tide would occur that afternoon.

"I think around three thirty," I said.

"Good," Kevin said. "We can paddle out to the sandbar right after lunch. I just hope the waves are as big today as they were Friday and Saturday."

I lowered my gaze and cleared my throat. Then I looked at Kevin. "I can't surf this afternoon. I'm water-skiing with a friend."

Kevin made a face. "Since when do you water-ski?"

"I haven't yet; he's going to teach me."

Kevin lowered his gaze to his cornflakes while he worked his jaw from side to side. Then he looked at me and said, "I don't understand why you made plans with someone else when you knew I was coming for the weekend."

Uh-oh.

"That's not how it happened," I said. "I made the plans on Monday, before I knew you were coming. If I'd known..."

Kevin's eyes narrowed. "Who *is* this guy, anyway?"

"His name is Lane; he's in my service club at school."

"You never mentioned him before. How come?"

I explained how I'd just known Lane a short time, how we'd worked together at the Civitan painting project, and how he'd surfed with me at the sandbar once. "He's a nice guy," I told Kevin, "and he's my only real friend at school."

Kevin rearranged his limbs in his dining chair while a vertical crease appeared between his eyebrows. Then he looked at me and said, "Are you fooling around with him? Is he...?"

"Of course not," I said. "We're just friends."

"This is supposed to be our weekend," Kevin said. "I was counting on it. Why don't you call your friend and cancel? Tell him something came up and you can't make it; he'll understand."

I wasn't sure what to do. I didn't want to hurt Kevin's feelings. And we'd had such a wonderful time the past two days. Why not enjoy one more? But then I thought about Lane and how much I liked spending time with him. Plus it wouldn't be fair of me to renege on a commitment I'd made to Lane well before Kevin called me on Thursday.

"I can't do that," I said to Kevin. "Lane and his parents are expecting me."

Kevin puckered one side of his face and shook his head. "Thanks a lot, Jesse. Thanks a whole lot."

"Don't be mad," I said, but I knew he was.

When Kevin rose from his chair, the legs scraped against our wooden floor. He took his bowl to the kitchen; I heard him rinse it in the sink. Then he strode into my bedroom and I heard a rustling of clothing. By the time I joined Kevin in my bedroom, he'd slipped into a pair of Bermuda shorts, and now he was stuffing his other belongings into the overnight bag he'd brought with him on Friday. His mouth was a thin line and his eyebrows were gathered.

"Are you leaving already?" I said.

He nodded.

"Why so early?" I said. "Mom and Lisa won't be home till noon. Until then, we'll have the house to ourselves; we can do whatever we want."

"No thanks," Kevin muttered while he closed the hasp on his bag. "You have fun with your buddy; I'll see you later."

Before I could reach for my own shorts, Kevin had brushed past me and headed for our home's front door. Moments later, I heard the roar of the Mustang's muffler. I stood there in my room, staring at my jelly-stained sheets and messed-up covers, and wondered to myself how long it might be before Kevin slept with me again. Had I screwed things up between us in a major way?

Chapter Twelve

LANE'S HOME WAS contemporary, a stucco-over-cinder-block house with a white tile roof and a yard that looked professionally landscaped. Waist-high crotons formed multicolored hedges that grew against the exterior walls. Two royal palms with waxy fronds towered above the house. The St. Augustine grass was emerald, mown and edged as neatly as pie slices. Inside, a central air-conditioning system kept things quiet and cool. My feet sunk into cut-pile carpet while Lane introduced me to his parents; they looked like two models in a department store advertisement.

Mr. Davis (first name Tom) was a few inches taller than me, with hair the same color as Lane's, but cut much shorter. When he shook my hand with a firm grip, his lips folded back to display his pearly teeth. He wore swim trunks and a T-shirt with a Bermuda hotel's logo on the chest. Lane's mom, Bev, looked almost young enough to be Lane's older sister. She wore a one-piece swimsuit, a tennis visor, and sandals. Her dark hair was pulled back into a ponytail, and when we she shook my hand, her palm was cool and light, like a sea breeze.

Sliding glass doors at the rear of the house offered a view of Boca Ciega Bay and a wooden dock with davits. The dock thrust about fifty feet into the bay. A fiberglass boat with an outboard engine the size of an oil drum floated next to the dock, secured by tether lines.

Lane was dressed like me: surfing baggies, flip-flops, and a T-shirt, only he'd hacked off the sleeves of his shirt to display his stringy biceps and triceps. While I helped him tote an ice chest to the dock, he chattered away.

"We'll ski where the water's surface is smooth, probably in the upper bay, for a couple of hours. There's an island there called Dog Leg Key. We'll anchor in the shallows there around three, so we can swim and have ourselves a snack. Then we'll get back to our dock no later than five. Sound good?"

The Davises' boat was a twenty-one footer with a center console where the wheel and throttle were located. The engine was a one-hundred-fifty-horsepower Evinrude. The boat's stainless steel brightwork gleamed and the blue canvas upholstery on the benches looked new. A pair of skis, a life jacket, and a ski rope rested on the foredeck.

While Lane and his mom cast off the dock lines, Mr. Davis stood at the boat's center console. He switched on the outboard engine, and then it rumbled as he eased the boat away from the dock at minimal speed. Once we were clear, he told everyone to find a seat. I sat next to Lane on a bench seat in front of the console, while Lane's mom joined her husband at the console's bench. The engine roared to life when Lane's dad eased the throttle forward. The boat's nose lifted, and after we "got up on plane," as Lane called it, we glided across the bay's glassy surface.

The wind tossed my hair about while the engine hummed. We passed homes with screened-in swimming pools and majestic sailboats with tall masts tethered to their docks. Plenty of other powerboats buzzed about the bay that afternoon, and each time we passed an oncoming boat, its occupants waved to us. We waved back. If we passed over another boat's wake, the nose of our boat would bounce and I'd grip the edge of our bench to steady myself.

To me, boating wasn't all that different from surfing. I liked the fluidity of the boat's movement and the feel of the wind on my cheeks. I savored the scent of the bay's briny air. After passing under Treasure Island's drawbridge, we continued northward until we reached an area near the Jungle Prada Pier, where Mr. Davis throttled down the engine.

"We like skiing in this area," Lane told me, "and not just 'cause the water's calm. Most days, there aren't many other boats around."

I glanced here and there, and I saw Lane was right. Other than a couple of boaters who had anchored and were fishing, I saw no other vessels around.

Lane turned to his parents. "Jesse hasn't skied before," he told them. "Why don't I go first so he can watch me? Then he can give it a try."

After Lane fastened the life jacket on, he picked up the skis and hopped off the rear of the boat (the "stern") with the skis under his arm. He slipped one foot into each ski's stirrup, and, while he bobbed in the water with his ski tips raised, his mom tied one end of the ski rope to a cleat at the stern. She tossed Lane the end of the rope with a handle on it.

With Lane a safe distance from the Evinrude, Mr. Davis putt-putted away from Lane until the ski rope was almost fully extended, a length of maybe seventy-five feet. While he did this, Mr. Davis explained a few things to me.

"For safety's sake, when a skier's in the water, one person in the boat should always keep his or her eyes on the skier. Right now, Bev will serve as our lookout. When Lane gives me a thumbs-up signal, I'll throttle up the engine.

"Now, here's the trick to getting out of the water and up on your skis: once the boat starts moving, don't try to pull yourself up onto your feet; you'll fall every time. Instead, let the *boat* pull you out of the water gradually. Once you're up, keep your knees bent and your eyes fixed on the boat. Don't look down at your feet, or you'll lose your balance."

I stood alongside Mr. Davis, looking back at Lane and holding on to a handrail on the console. When Lane gave the thumbs-up, Mr. Davis shoved the throttle forward, and the engine roared. The boat took off, and very quickly Lane emerged from the water, gripping the ski rope's handle in both his hands. Sunlight reflected off his wet arms and shoulders, and a grin painted his face. Right away, he began cutting across the engine's V-shaped wake, going back and forth over the wake's waves, much like snow skiers I'd seen coming down the side of a mountain in an Olympic slalom event.

"See how his knees are bent?" Mr. Davis hollered, so I could hear over the engine's roar.

I nodded.

"That helps absorb the shocks from the wake when he travels over it."

We traveled in a horse-track pattern, going a quarter mile or so before turning in an arc, then going a quarter mile in the opposite direction. After three laps, Lane waved a hand, and Mr. Davis slowed the motor. Lane dropped into the water; he let go of the ski rope, and then his mom gathered in the rope while we circled back to pick up Lane.

Moments later, *I* was in the warm and placid water, bobbing in my life vest with my feet inserted into the skis' stirrups and the tips of my skis pointing skyward. I'd placed the rope between the skis, the way Lane had shown me. When I gave Mrs. Davis the thumbs-up, her husband accelerated. I felt the boat's pull on the rope, but then I forgot what Mr. Davis had told me. I tried to lift myself upward by pulling on the rope's handle, and right away, I crashed into the water after losing my grip on the handle. One ski tore loose from my foot, and then I swallowed a good amount of bay water before I surfaced, coughing like crazy and feeling both stupid and clumsy.

Mr. Davis circled the boat around so I could grab the rope's handle again. After I put my foot back in the loose ski's stirrup, I positioned myself as before, in a seated position with my ski tips skyward. When I gave the thumbs-up and the motor roared, I made the same stupid mistake I'd made the first time: I pulled on the rope in a vain attempt to rise.

Down I went.

When the boat circled back for me again, I looked at Lane and shook my head. "Maybe I'm not cut out for this," I hollered over the engine's muttering.

"Nonsense," Lane hollered back. "Everyone screws up at first; it's part of learning. Just try to remember: let the *boat* pull you up."

Right after I gave Mrs. Davis my third thumbs-up, I closed my eyes and spoke out loud to myself. "Let the *boat* pull you up, dumbass. Let the *boat* pull you up."

Fifteen seconds later, I stood on the skis while screaming across the water's surface. I felt like I was flying. On the boat, Lane waved his hands and pumped his fist. Then he pointed to his knees and made a squatting motion.

Bend your knees, Jesse.

I bent my knees. Then, after I turned my hips, I began crossing over the wake's waves. It seemed like I was driving across a set of railroad tracks each time I did so. I felt my knees absorb the shocks, as Mr. Davis had said.

After two laps, my shoulders ached and my thighs felt wobbly, I guess because I was using different muscles than I normally did when surfing or mowing lawns. I waved at Mrs. Davis, and then the boat slowed. I let go of the rope handle, then settled into the water, feeling somewhat amazed by the fact I'd actually managed to water-ski. Who'd have guessed?

The rest of the afternoon sped by. Mr. Davis took his turn in the water, followed by Lane's mom. Both looked as comfortable on skis as they might be on their living room sofa. I tried to imagine *my* mom skimming along the water's surface, but couldn't. She barely knew how to swim. And then I thought about the huge difference between Lane's upbringing and mine. Lane was a child of the middle class, the scion of an athletic family with looks as well as physical prowess.

Me? I was a skinny working-class kid with few physical talents.

Still, it felt good to spend time with a family like the Davises. When we anchored at Dog Leg Key, a sand spit with a mangrove thicket growing in its center, we all waded to shore with the ice cooler and a canvas beach bag filled with chips and crackers. Then we drank from bottles of cold soda. We gobbled chips while sitting on the island's sandy shore. I answered Lane's parents' questions about myself: my family, my classes at school, my lawn-care business, and even my car. I thought it was nice they showed an interest in my life when they really didn't have to.

Lane's mom said, "Lane tells us you're in National Honor Society." And after I nodded, she said, "What are your college plans?"

I rocked my head from side to side. "I'm not sure the university is something I could afford. Like I said, my dad's out of the picture, and money's tight at our house. Maybe I'll attend community college. That way I could live at home and keep my yard-care business going."

Mrs. Davis glanced at Lane, then returned her gaze to me. "Community college is fine, of course, but you'd get a better education up in Gainesville, and not just in the classroom. It's the variety of people you'd meet there that make the difference."

Lane's dad nodded. "Plus you're on your own at the university; it teaches you independence."

Lane groaned. "Mom, Dad," he said, "you shouldn't preach to Jesse." He turned to me and rolled his eyes. "They're *always* telling me this stuff."

Mrs. Davis placed her hand on Lane's forearm. "It's only because we want the best for you, sweetie. You know that."

Lane gazed into his lap and nodded. "Still, let's give the college talk a rest today. We're supposed to be having fun, alright?"

I felt a little awkward at that moment, like I was intruding on Lane's family's private issues, so I didn't say anything. I only poked at the sand with the end of a driftwood stick I'd found until Lane nudged my shoulder. "Let's take a swim," he said, and moments later, we stood up to our waists in the bay, about fifty feet from the key's shore. We had swum out there, and now our hair was plastered to our skulls and beads of bay water glistened on our shoulders.

"Sorry about my parents' lecturing," Lane said, just softly enough that they couldn't hear him. "It's like they can't help themselves."

"I don't mind," I said. "They mean well, and what they're saying is probably right: the university's my best option. But paying for it's a problem."

Lane shrugged. "Talk to the guidance counselor at school. She might be able to help with that."

I lowered my gaze and nodded.

"I'll do that," I said.

WHEN I RETURNED home from the Davises' house, my sister studied a chemistry text at our dining table while my mom rattled pots and pans in the kitchen.

The first thing I said to each of them was, "Has Kevin called?"

They both shook their heads, and then I headed for the bathroom to get myself clean. I stood beneath the showerhead, feeling warm water pound my shoulders and chest, while I pondered the afternoon I'd just spent with Lane and his folks. All three of them had treated me like I was part of their family and not just a guest. And when I left their place, both Lane and his dad shook my hand. Mrs. Davis gave me a hug.

"Come see us again," she told me. "You're always welcome here."

But despite the fact I'd enjoyed the hell out of myself with the Davises, I felt guilty about the way things had ended with Kevin that morning. I'd hurt Kevin's feelings, I thought, and now I wondered if I had ruined all the progress we'd made in our relationship since the day Kevin told me his father was dead. Since then, Kevin had been less guarded about his feelings for me and more affectionate. In my mind, we were boyfriends now, and yet I had chosen water-skiing with Lane over surfing with Kevin.

No wonder Kevin was angry with me.

After I got myself dressed, I slipped out the front door and strolled to a phone booth on the corner of Gulf Boulevard. Traffic swished by as I dumped a nickel and dime into coin slots before dialing Kevin's number. I chewed my lips while the Corrigans' phone rang once, twice, and a third time before Kevin's mom answered.

After I told her it was me, I asked for Kevin.

"He's over at a neighbor's right now," she said, and right away, my mood plunged. I was pretty certain which neighbor Kevin was visiting, and I was fairly sure what the two of them were up to as well. Kevin, I knew, was exacting his revenge on me, and I was paying for my disloyalty in a very hurtful manner. Someone else was touching Kevin the way only I should touch him, and it was my fault; I had brought it upon myself.

"Will you have him call me when he gets home?" I asked in a shaky voice.

After Mrs. Corrigan said yes and I said thanks, the conversation ended. I stood there in the phone booth, just staring through the glass at passing traffic and feeling as blue as I'd ever been in my life.

Kevin, of course, did not return my call. When Thursday night rolled around, I camped out in our living room with a textbook in my lap that I couldn't even concentrate on because I was too nervous. I sat and stared at the silent telephone on our desk. I waited from seven thirty till nine p.m., but Kevin never called. He didn't call when the weekend arrived either.

Saturday, while I mowed and edged lawns, I felt hollow inside, like someone had scooped the internal organs out of my body and tossed them into a trashcan. I made lackluster conversations with my customers when they paid me while trying my best to keep our talks to a minimum. I even declined Spencer's offer of a Coke and a Marlboro when I tended his parents' yard. The only person I felt like speaking to was Kevin. I craved his presence and the sound of his voice, and I yearned for his piney scent.

Then do something about it.

Saturday night, right after my sister and I cleaned up the dinner dishes, I dressed in good school clothes and penny loafers. I combed my hair, brushed my teeth, and gargled with mouthwash. I dabbed cologne on my neck, then told my mom I was going out for a while, to spend time with my Civitan buddies, but my story was a lie.

I climbed into the Dart and fired up the engine. Then I drove to Bishop Keating High School, only stopping along the way to buy a pack of L&Ms. By the time I arrived at the school, darkness had fallen. Lights inside the gymnasium glowed and the parking lot was jammed with at least a hundred cars, some new and shiny, others older with faded paint jobs and dented bumpers. I drove up and down the rows until I found what I was looking for: Kevin's car. I parked in a space fairly close to the Mustang, then exited the Dart.

Crickets chirped in live oaks growing in the parking lot's perimeter. The words of a tune popular at the time, "The Letter" by Neon Rainbow, wafted from the gymnasium's open clerestory windows. I leaned against my car's front fender and lit a cigarette with a match. I blew streams of smoke like a dragon while keeping my gaze fixed on Kevin's car.

I wasn't really sure what I was doing at Bishop Keating or what I would say if I saw Kevin, but I felt I belonged exactly where I was. Kevin was my prey. So, I waited and smoked, and then I waited some more. Each time I glanced at my wristwatch, it seemed like the workings of the watch were gummed up with glue.

Every five minutes or so, a couple emerged from the gym's open double doors, and then the building's interior lights would cast a yellow rectangle of light onto the sidewalk leading from the gym to the parking lot. The boys were dressed much as I was while the girls wore white blouses and dark skirts hemmed at the knee. The couples almost always strolled to one car or another, and then, after they climbed into the front or rear seat, I was fairly certain what went on in the shadows.

A half hour passed. I had already smoked four cigarettes and my throat felt like I'd taken sandpaper to it. I was thirsty as hell too. So I walked to the gymnasium in search of a water fountain, and just when I approached the gym's open doors, two couples emerged from inside. We all came face to face with one another. The girls and one of the boys I didn't know. But the other boy was Kevin. As soon as his gaze met mine, he knitted his eyebrows, then looked away. He and the girl with him brushed past me without saying a word. Both couples walked in the direction of Kevin's car.

I stood at the gym doors, flexing my fingers at my hips while my heart pounded and my vision blurred. What should I do? Kevin hadn't even acknowledged my presence when he saw me. He treated me like I was invisible or maybe something to be ashamed of.

I entered the gym, where throngs of teenagers, all dressed very much the same, swayed to the beat of a tune by the Supremes, "My World is Empty Without You." The music blasted from a pair of speakers taller than me. The room was warm because so many people were in there and most were moving about. Clumps of adults stood here and there, the women wearing dresses and heels, the men white shirts and ties, and I presumed they were chaperones. I bought an admission ticket for seventy-five cents from a lady with close-cropped hair and horn-rimmed glasses who sat behind a card table. Then I found the men's room, where I splashed my face with cold water at a sink. I drank from the tap till my throat didn't feel so parched. Then I dried my face with a paper towel. When I studied my reflection in the mirror above the sink, my eyes had a stricken look to them, as though I were in pain, and in a sense, I was. Not *physical* pain but the emotional variety.

After I ambled back into the gym, I stood at the edge of the dance floor, feeling utterly out of place. I didn't know a single soul in the room. I might as well have been in a foreign country. All around me, kids were grinning and chattering away. Two boys in black letterman's sweaters with gold Ks sewn on the pockets sold cola in paper cups. I bought a cup for a quarter. Then I tapped a toe while I sipped the fizzy liquid and chewed on chipped ice.

I figured I had three options at that point. First, I could remain inside the gym in the hope that Kevin would return, but it was possible he wouldn't. Second, I could leave campus and go back home, which seemed like a chickenshit move. Kevin had already seen me and he knew why I was there. Leaving right now would make me look cowardly. Third, I could go to Kevin's Mustang and ask to speak with him, which I thought was probably my best choice. At least *something* would happen, and what did I have to lose?

After I tossed my cola cup into a trashcan, I squared my shoulders and headed for the exit doors. Outside, the temperature was mercifully cooler, but I still felt dampness in my armpits as I strode toward the Mustang. My pulse drummed inside my head. When I got to Kevin's car, the windows were rolled down but the interior dome light wasn't lit, and I found it hard to see what was going on inside.

After I placed my hands on the driver's door sill, I squinted and looked inside. Kevin held his girl in his arms. The two were kissing and the girl's eyes were closed. One of her hands rested on Kevin's thigh. In the backseat, much the same was going on, so no one even noticed my presence until I cleared my throat. Both couples separated like I'd zapped them with a cattle prod.

"Jesus *Christ*, Jesse," Kevin hollered when he saw it was me. "What are you doing here?"

I shifted my weight from one leg to the other while I pondered what I should say. In the meantime, the girl in the backseat said, "Who *is* that?"

"Just someone I know," Kevin said.

I cleared my throat again. Then I told Kevin, "I need to talk to you."

"I'm busy right now."

"It'll only take a few minutes."

The girl seated next to Kevin whispered something in his ear, and then Kevin told me, "Okay, but let's make it quick."

Kevin left his car. Then we walked out of earshot of the folks in the Mustang. After we both leaned our butts against a car's fender, I offered Kevin an L&M, and we lit up. The ashes on our cigarettes glowed in the darkness while crickets continued to chirp.

"Are you mad at me?" I asked.

"What does it matter if I am?" Kevin said.

"Look, I'm sorry. I should've canceled the skiing and stayed with you. It's just Lane's the first new friend I've had in a long time and—"

Kevin hissed. "That makes him more important than me?"

When I squeezed Kevin's shoulder, he shrugged off my hand. "Don't touch me like that," he said. "Not here."

I glanced over at the Mustang, then looked at Kevin again. "I need to see you," I said. "After the dance, why don't you come to my place; you can spend the night. Tomorrow I'll lend you a pair of surfing trunks. Then we can hit the sandbar; we can share my board."

Kevin drew on his cigarette. Thirty seconds passed before he spoke. "I'll think about it, but I'm not promising anything. In the meantime, you need to get out of here. What you and I do at your house is one thing. My life at school is another, understand?"

I nodded, feeling like some family's idiot child they always kept locked in a bedroom so no one else could see him. "Okay," I said. "If that's what you want."

After Kevin dropped his cigarette onto the asphalt, he crushed it with his toe.

"That's what I want," he said.

Chapter Thirteen

OF COURSE KEVIN didn't come to my house the night I visited Bishop Keating, nor did he call or otherwise contact me in the weeks following, and after a while, I came to believe that our relationship, whatever it had been, was through. In the Bishop Keating parking lot, Kevin had made it clear that his life was strictly compartmentalized. At school he was one person, at my house he was another, and I wasn't a person he wished to be seen with when his Catholic friends were around.

By now, I saw Kevin's jealous snit over Lane for what it truly was, and it wasn't the type of jealousy that stemmed from love. Kevin was only angry that I didn't plan my Sunday around him, when he had nothing better to do than surf with me. He expected me to make myself available to him whenever he wanted, but I had no right to expect the same from him. And how fair was that?

Of course I still craved Kevin's physical attentions. My sexual hunger seemed to grow stronger every month, but so did my self-respect, and maybe I no longer needed Kevin's approval in order to feel good about myself.

The second Friday in November, Lane's parents took me and Lane to Cocoa Beach, on Florida's east coast, with our surfboards strapped to the roof of the Davises' Chevrolet station wagon. They rented two rooms, one for themselves and the other for me and Lane, at a nice motel with coconut palms, a swimming pool, and shuffleboard courts. The motel was right on the beach and within walking distance of the Cocoa Beach Pier, a wooden structure extending two hundred yards into the Atlantic.

When we arrived at the motel, the sun had just set over the Banana River to the west. Lane and I visited the beach, where several surfers bobbed on their boards, just north of the pier. The waves rolling in were far larger than those at the Treasure Island sandbar; most were shoulder height, and I licked my lips with anticipation. Tomorrow, Lane and I would rise when the sun did. We'd wax our boards and paddle out, and as I watched one surfer ride the face of a slablike wave, I wondered just how well I could handle the pier's larger swell.

Friday night, Lane and I walked down a sidewalk abutting A-1-A. The four-lane highway buzzed with traffic while an onshore breeze tossed our hair into our faces. We visited an amusement parlor where we played a few games of pool, and we chattered away while we did so. By now each of us seemed thoroughly comfortable with the other, and we never really ran out of things to talk about.

Of course I didn't tell Lane about my relationship with Kevin. Nor did I allow myself to think of Lane in a sexual way. He was good-looking, of course. If he'd made a pass at me, I would have jumped at the chance to touch him. But he had never said anything or made a single gesture that indicated a sexual interest in me. We were friends, nothing more, and I was fine with it.

Back at the motel, after we undressed, we climbed into our respective twin beds. Our surfboards leaned against a wall; they stood on end and looked like a pair of tombstones. After Lane extinguished the lamp on the bureau between us, we lay beneath the covers, and then Lane spoke of a vacation his family took in July each year.

"We always rent a cabin in the Blue Ridge Mountains, up in North Carolina, for two weeks. The temperature's cool there in summer, but the sky is sunny. Every day, we do a different hike. There are waterfalls and rapids, things you'd never see in Florida. And we always rent horses for an afternoon. Ever ride one?"

"Never."

"Maybe this summer you can come with us. You'd have a good time."

I didn't know what to say. Until that day, I'd never been farther from St. Petersburg than Ft. Lauderdale. The thought of traveling to North Carolina seemed like a trip to the moon.

"That would be great," I told Lane.

I found it hard to fall asleep that night. I was keyed up about being in Cocoa Beach and staying in a motel room with Lane and also about the possibility I might vacation with the Davises later in the year. It all seemed like a dream to me. I lay in my bed and listened to Lane's soft snoring, and I wondered what Kevin might say if he saw where I was and who I was with.

Kevin, I knew, had never enjoyed the type of friendship I had developed with Lane. In fact, by Kevin's admission *I* was his only real friend, and really, what kind of a screwed-up friendship did we have? I was someone Kevin only came to when he was bored, or horny, or when he felt threatened by life. Otherwise, he could do without me just fine.

Wasn't it time I did fine without Kevin?

"HOLY CRAP," LANE said in a half whisper.

We stood on the shore, just north of the pier while the sun's upper edge appeared on the eastern horizon, providing just enough light for us to see a wave break, about halfway between shore and the pier's end. The wave was bigger than those we'd seen the previous afternoon. Already two guys had paddled out on their boards; they bobbed on the Atlantic's surface while staring eastward and shading their foreheads with their hands.

Above us, stars still appeared in the brightening sky and a half-moon was sinking toward the Banana River on the barrier island's opposite side. A light breeze ruffled our hair while we watched one surfer turn the nose of his board toward shore. Behind him, another wave rose like a liquid wall. The surfer paddled furiously, chopping at the water with his hands, and then the wave lifted him. He popped up on his feet with his left foot forward and his right trailing. Then, after he turned the nose of his board, he skimmed across the wave's face with his arms extended and his knees bent.

"Amazing," I said to Lane. "Think we can do it?"

He looked at me and shrugged. "I guess there's only one way to find out."

We walked our boards out till we were waist deep in the chilly water. Foam remnants from broken waves swirled around us. We waited for a lull in the arrival of waves so our paddle-out would take less effort, and after a minute or so, a respite came. We hopped onto our boards, lay our stomachs, and paddled like crazy until we reached the "outside," a spot just a little beyond where the morning's waves broke.

We both sat on our boards, bobbing with the ocean's roll and looking eastward for oncoming waves. By now the sun was fully above the horizon. It looked like a fiery coin, and the glare it produced made me squint while I savored the ocean's briny aroma. Off in the distance, a manta ray the size of queen-size blanket leapt from the ocean with its whiplike tail twitching and water streaming off its skin. Then it came crashing down, spewing water everywhere.

Lane pointed eastward. "Here comes one," he hollered, and then we both watched the wave approach. It looked even bigger than the ones we'd seen from shore, with a glassy face and a curling lip that reflected the sun rays. We both turned the noses of our boards toward shore, then began to paddle. I heard the roar of the wave behind me—it sounded like a freight train—and then it lifted me. My board took off like a rocket while I popped up into a crouch with my arms extended. I shifted my hips for only two seconds, and my board turned into the wave's face. Lane had done the same, and now both of us zoomed along the wave's face like a pair of snow skiers screaming down a slope.

Lane lifted his face; he hooted at the sky like a Comanche, and I did as well.

Our ride probably lasted ten second before the wave petered out near shore, and both of us fell from our boards and into the shallow water. I felt so exhilarated I could barely speak. The ride had seemed like a religious ritual incorporating some sort of narcotic. Lane and I stood there, holding onto the rails of our boards, just staring at each other while huge grins painted our faces. Water streamed from our hair; it glistened on our shoulders.

"Can you believe this?" Lane finally asked.

I shook my head. "That wave felt like a locomotive," I said. "It came up so quickly I didn't have time to get scared. I just let it grab me, and then I stood up."

Lane nodded while he pushed wet hair away from his face. Then he looked at me. "We have to come over here more often."

We surfed about three hours that morning, until the waves subsided and our arms were rubbery. Several times I'd misjudged the size of a wave I tried to catch; I positioned myself too far forward on my board. Each time I did, the nose of my board went under, and so did I. I found myself spinning underwater, and each time, when I finally surfaced, I coughed up sea water like crazy.

Still, I didn't let myself get discouraged. My first ride had hooked me like heroin, and all I wanted was more waves. If half drowning myself was the price I had to pay for those waves, I'd gladly do so.

When we finally came ashore and returned to our room, both of us showered and changed into dry clothes. This was the first time I saw

Lane naked, and though I had promised myself I would never think about him in a sexual way, I couldn't help myself. His broad shoulders tapered to a narrow waist, his chest was defined, and his creamy buttocks had a nice curve to them.

There in the motel room, I had to tear my gaze from Lane's body before I got stiff.

Get yourself under control, Lockhart.

After lunch at a cafe, Lane's parents took us to the Kennedy Space Center, where we looked at the Mercury rockets NASA had used in its early launches, and also a Saturn V rocket identical to one launched in an unmanned flight, only days before. The Saturn was *huge*, longer than three football fields, and I could not imagine how such a large and heavy object could actually launch into space.

That night, we dined on seafood at an outdoor restaurant overlooking the Banana River. I had fresh grouper stuffed with crabmeat, and I don't think I'd ever eaten something so delicious. I don't know why. Maybe because we dined outdoors, or perhaps because it felt so good being part of the Davis family's weekend.

At the end of the evening, when Lane and I climbed into our respective beds and Lane turned out the light, I lay between my cool sheets and replayed the events of the day inside my head. How could things have gone more perfectly? The surfing was fantastic, the trip to the Space Center was a treat, and—

A vision of Lane naked and drying himself with a towel stole into my thoughts, and I couldn't help myself; I reached between my legs and brought myself to orgasm as quietly as I could. After I cleaned myself up with the sheet, I rolled onto my side. A slice of light from a corridor fixture entered our room from the edges of the drapes, and I could just make out Lane's facial features: his straight nose, jutting cheekbones, and cleft chin. His hair was fanned out across his pillow.

I turned onto my back and stared at the ceiling.

He's your friend, Lockhart, and that's all he is.

Accept it.

Chapter Fourteen

THE THURSDAY FOLLOWING my trip to Cocoa Beach, our desk phone rang at precisely eight p.m. I sat at our dining table, working on an essay for my English class, and when I heard the phone, I glanced at my wristwatch. Right away I knew who was calling.

My sister was babysitting for our neighbors and my mom was playing bridge with neighbors, so I was alone. When I answered the phone, I didn't even say hello.

"What do you want, Kevin?"

"How did you know it was me?"

I rolled my eyes. "It doesn't matter," I said. "Just tell me why you're calling."

"I thought maybe I'd spend this weekend at your house, if you'd like that."

I shifted my weight from one leg to the other while I twisted the phone cord around my finger. "Don't you have a football game Friday night?"

Kevin cleared his throat before he answered. "I injured my knee last week. I can't play for the rest of the season."

"What about the dance on Saturday? What about the girls from St. Mary's?"

"I can't dance either, not right now because I limp pretty badly."

I could almost feel steam pouring out of my ears. "Listen," I said, "the last time I saw you, I finally figured something out: you're ashamed of me and what we do when we're alone. And I'm not important, either; I'm just somebody you see when you have nothing better to do."

"That's not true, I—"

"Why don't you find some other queer to use? Go see your neighbor; maybe he's more desperate than I am."

I slammed the phone's receiver down on the cradle and stood there staring into space while my chest rose and fell. I felt a mixture of pride and regret: pride for finally standing up to Kevin, and regret for passing up an opportunity to have sex with him.

Well, what's done is done.

I returned to the dining table and got busy with my essay. I chewed my pencil's eraser while I tried to focus on my work instead of Kevin, but it was hard not to think of him and the sex we might have enjoyed on Friday and Saturday nights if I'd been more receptive to his request. Many weeks had passed since I'd last touched Kevin, and now my hormones were raging. I could almost smell Kevin's piney scent when I imagined the two of us moving against each other between my bedsheets.

Perhaps twenty minutes passed, and then I heard a familiar sound: the rumble of a Mustang's muffler. I glanced out a window in time to see Kevin's headlights illuminate our garage door. I sat in my chair, as still as a mannequin, while I listened to Kevin exit the Mustang. Moments later, he rapped on our front porch's screened door.

I flicked on the porch lights and met Kevin at the screened door. I kept telling myself, *Don't lose control. Stand your ground and don't let him take advantage of you.*

I gazed at Kevin through the screen, but I didn't invite him inside; I just stood there staring at him while he looked up at me from the stoop. I heard his breath whistle in his nose while his chest rose and fell. He wore a Keating sweatshirt and blue jeans, and the glow from our porch lights reflected in his yellow hair. He leaned against an aluminum cane with a rubber tip on its lower end.

"Can I come in?" he said.

"What for?"

His gaze left mine for a moment, and then he returned it to me. "We should talk," he said. "I know you're mad, but—"

"You're damned right I'm mad, and I have every right to be after the way you acted at the dance. Do you know how it made me feel?"

He shook his head.

"Like a piece of dog shit. That's how."

Kevin lowered his chin while he cleared his throat. Then he looked at me again. "I'm sorry, okay? I shouldn't have done what I did. Our friendship's more important than those kids in my car."

I hissed and shook my head. "If our friendship's so important, then how come I haven't heard from you in what...a month? It's the same thing, over and over with you: I see you a few times, and then you fall off the radar. No phone calls, no visits, just...nothing. It's like I don't exist."

Kevin raised his voice a notch while he gestured with his hands like a lawyer pleading his case to a jury. "You don't know how busy I am, and not just with football. I have school and my counseling sessions. And even though my dad's gone, Mom still needs my help around the house. I do the yard work and clean the pool, all that stuff."

I crossed my arms at my chest, then raised my voice as well. "But now that your leg's screwed up and you can't play football or dance, you'll have plenty of time for me. Is that how it works?"

Kevin kept his gaze fixed on mine while he let out his breath. "Are you going to invite me in or not?"

"I have homework to finish."

"I won't stay long; a half hour tops."

When I motioned Kevin inside, he winced when he made the step up from the stoop to the porch. He lurched into the house like Quasimodo while his cane clunked against the floorboards.

"Jesus," I said, "you really *are* hurt."

He nodded, then gritted his teeth while he sat down on our sofa. "They think I tore something called an ACL," he said. "The doctor told me I might never play football again."

I sat on the sofa alongside Kevin. "They can't fix it?" I asked.

He shook his head. "If the knee doesn't heal by itself, there's not much they can do."

We sat there for several moments, listening to the sound of traffic pass on Gulf Boulevard. Neither of us looked at the other. Kevin asked where my mom and sister were, and right after I explained, he placed his hand on my thigh. His gaze met mine and he raised his eyebrows.

Don't do it.

I kept my gaze fixed on Kevin's while I shook my head. "I don't have the time," I said.

Kevin moved his hand to my crotch. He gave me a squeeze, and right away, I stiffened, something he most certainly felt. "It won't take us long," he said. "You know that."

I looked down at his hand and pulled it from between my legs. "Sorry," I said, "but you can't have me."

"Why?"

"I already explained: I won't let you treat me like crap any longer. Either we're boyfriends—and that means I come first—or we're not. You need to make a choice and stick to it."

Kevin gazed into his lap while he rubbed his lips together.

"You don't have to decide right now," I said. "Take your time. But you can't stay here this weekend, not without making a commitment first. It's the way things have to be from now on."

Kevin bobbed his chin, but he still wouldn't look at me, and I could almost hear his brain fluids churn. Finally he turned his gaze to mine, and he cleared his throat.

"All right," he said. "You win. Just tell me what I have to do."

I DIDN'T LET Kevin touch me that night, but we agreed he would spend the weekend with me.

"I won't be able to surf," he said. "Even walking is painful, so don't expect a whole lot from me."

The next day, Kevin showed at my place around five p.m. with his overnight bag and his cane. My mom and sister fawned over him like he'd been the victim of a heinous crime or a war injury. They listened raptly while Kevin explained what had happened the previous Friday night.

"A receiver I defended managed to catch a pass. When I tackled him, he was still in midair. He fell on top of me and then my leg got twisted. Right away, I knew something was wrong. It felt like someone had jabbed a knife into the side of my knee."

At the dinner table that night, my mom told Kevin he needn't help with the dishes, but Kevin insisted he would. "I'm not *that* crippled," he said, and soon we stood side by side at the sink. I washed while Kevin dried and put things away, just like we had that summer when Kevin lived with us.

We passed the evening playing gin rummy with my mom and sister, then watched the CBS Friday Night Movie, an Alfred Hitchcock thriller called *Torn Curtain*. To be honest, I felt bored and restless. Normally, Kevin and I would have left the house to walk on the beach or maybe we'd have played mini-golf. We might have fished at the John's Pass Bridge. But none of that would happen, not with Kevin's knee injury in the mix, and I slowly began to realize just how serious the situation was.

Thankfully our sex that night didn't disappoint. Kevin, of course, was limited in the positions he could assume, due to his knee and the elastic brace he wore on it. But we got creative and it all worked out amazingly well. I felt like a starving man who'd wandered into a banquet hall. I couldn't get enough of Kevin's body, and when it was over, I lay beside him on the sweaty sheet. I listened to him breathe while a breeze sang in the needles of the Australian pine beyond the windows.

"What'll I do if this knee doesn't heal?" Kevin asked me. "If I can't play ball or dance, I'll be a nobody, just like one of those kids at school who no one notices or cares about."

"*I'll* still care about you," I said.

Kevin ran his fingers through my hair, then kissed my cheek. "Thanks for letting me stay here this weekend; it means a lot."

Kevin's words took me back to that night on the beach when he'd told me he wished he could live at my home forever. Back then, his words had swept me off my feet, but I wasn't fourteen and innocent anymore. I'd been down this path with Kevin too many times to think more of his words than I should. Kevin was vulnerable right now, as he had been after his mom's surgery or when his dad died. I thought back to the night when I'd visited the Keating campus and how awful I'd felt after Kevin walked away from me, and now I knew I would never let Kevin hurt me that way again.

Enjoy the moment, Lockhart, but don't expect a whole lot more. This may be all you'll ever get from him.

Saturday morning, I woke up shivering. A cold front had swept across central Florida during the night, and when I checked the thermometer on my bedroom wall, it said the room's temperature had plunged into the low fifties. Kevin lay next to me on his back, and I snuggled as close to him as possible so I could savor his body heat. The time was around seven and the sun had already risen. In the kitchen, my mom banged pots and pans. I smelled freshly brewed coffee and the pleasant scent of bacon frying.

I smooched Kevin's shoulder, and then his eyes fluttered open. After his gaze met mine, he ruffled my hair, and I was just about to kiss Kevin on the mouth when Mom's voice rang out.

"Jesse and Kevin, you boys need to get up. Breakfast goes on the table in ten minutes."

I rolled my eyes. "All right, Mom," I hollered. We both shivered when we crawled from beneath the covers and slipped into our clothes.

I had three lawns to care for that day, and though Kevin accompanied me to each job, he wasn't able to help much. You can't run a mower or a power edger when you're leaning against a cane. You can't rake leaves or hoe weeds. The best Kevin managed was hedge trimming. We both wore blue jeans and flannel shirts, and a steady breeze tossed our hair to and fro as we worked.

When we groomed the yard at Spencer's home, Kevin joined Spencer on the back door stoop. The two smoked Marlboros and chatted, about what I couldn't hear. After I finished the job, I wheeled my mower home while Kevin hobbled alongside me, pulling the edger behind him.

When I told Kevin how Spencer had made sexual advances at me, Kevin snickered and shook his head. "He's not shy, is he?"

I looked at Kevin and frowned. "Don't tell me..."

Kevin nodded while he pulled a scrap of paper from his pocket. "He gave me his phone number."

"What did you say?"

"I told him I had a girlfriend. Then he asked me about you; he wanted to know if you were gay."

Shit.

I told Kevin about the day I'd purchased the tube of jelly at the Rexall, when Spencer stood behind the register. "I think he's onto me," I said, "or at least he suspects."

Kevin shrugged. "I told him you were straight, but why do you care what he thinks anyway?"

I grimaced and shook my head. "I don't want him spreading rumors. People in this neighborhood gossip like crazy, and I don't want them talking about me."

Kevin's cane dragged along the concrete as we walked. "Have you ever thought about moving someplace where you could just be yourself, like New York? I hear people there don't even care if you're queer."

I made a face. Me leave Florida?

"It gets too cold in New York during winter," I said. "I don't think I'd like it."

"But you and I could live there together," Kevin said, "after we finish high school. No one would think twice about it if we did."

Kevin's remark jolted me so hard I felt like he'd knocked the wind out of me. My voice squeaked when I said, "Are you seriously thinking about that?"

"Sure," Kevin said. "Why not?"

I stopped pushing my mower. Then I placed my hands on my hips. Kevin stopped walking too. I looked at him. Then I said, "I don't understand you sometimes. A month back you told me to go away. I didn't hear from you again until two days ago, and now you're thinking we should live together?"

Kevin kneaded his cane's handle while he looked over my shoulder at something. "It's just an idea, Jesse."

"You keep jerking me around and it's driving me nuts. Make up your mind about what you really want from me, and then stick to it for once."

Kevin looked at me and scowled. He swatted the air with his hand. "Forget what I said, okay? I didn't know you'd get all angry like this."

I wasn't letting him off *that* easily.

"But don't you see? I have a *right* to be angry. I'd like nothing more than to live with you, but I don't think it'll ever happen."

"Why not?"

I hissed and shook my head. "Because you won't *let* it happen, that's why."

We walked the rest of the way home without saying another word, and as we walked I told myself, *If you had any balls you'd tell him to pack up his things and go home.* But of course I didn't. Our sex the night before had been wonderful, and I was too weak and needy to pass up another round with Kevin.

Sunday afternoon, I took Kevin for a long drive in my Dart, all the way from Treasure Island to Clearwater Beach, a distance of eighteen miles, one way. We drove on four-lane Gulf Boulevard, passing through beach towns like Redington Shores, Belleair Beach, and Indian Shores. This was the pre-condominium era, and most buildings we passed were single-family homes, mom-and-pop motels, luncheonettes, and convenience stores. The day was sunny and cool. We both wore blue jeans, sweatshirts, and sneakers. Kevin's cane leaned against the front seat, right next to him, as though it were part of him now. I had the radio switched on, and the Beatles' song "Lucy in the Sky with Diamonds" blasted from the speaker.

I stole a glance at Kevin from the corner of my eye. The passenger window was lowered and wind rushing through the car ruffled his hair. His arm rested on the door sill and he tapped a finger along with the music.

The evening before, I had swallowed my anger at Kevin's casual suggestion that we live together one day. We spent Saturday night at a movie theater on St. Pete Beach, watching *The Dirty Dozen,* an action film set in WWII Europe, with an all-star cast including Lee Marvin, Trini Lopez, and Charles Bronson. The theater was crowded with couples on dates, so we weren't able to get affectionate during the movie. But Kevin held my hand on the drive home, and I knew something good awaited me before the evening's end.

By the time we got home, the hour was past eleven and both my mom and sister were already in bed. After Kevin and I used the bathroom, we headed for my room and locked the door. Moments later, we writhed beneath the covers, and I was so horny I couldn't keep my hands off Kevin, not even for a second. Twice he told me to change position because I was hurting his knee.

Afterward, while I lay spoon-style with my back to Kevin and his arm draped around my waist, I tried to imagine how it would feel to fall asleep in his arms every night. *Hell,* I told myself, *I* would *live in stinking New York City if it meant having Kevin all the time.* But I knew better; I was pretty sure he'd never have the courage to share living quarters with me.

Now, as we reached Sand Key in my car, I parked in a lot just south of the drawbridge at Clearwater Pass. We sat there watching pleasure boats bob in the water, many occupied by folks using fishing poles. Sunlight reflected off waves smacking the seawall on the opposite side of the pass. I left the radio on, and the Doors' song "Light My Fire" played. I had seen Joel Brodsky's photos of the band's shirtless singer, Jim Morrison, and I thought Morrison looked pretty damned sexy with his sleek muscles and pouting lips. I found his syrupy voice seductive as well. Was it possible he might be gay?

Kevin broke into my reverie. He kept his gaze on the windshield while he spoke.

"I've been thinking about what you said yesterday, and I guess maybe I don't always understand myself or why I do what I do."

I looked at him and crinkled my forehead, then switched off the radio. "Explain, please."

Kevin shifted his butt in the car seat. "The way I behaved at the dance, the night you came to Keating, wasn't right. But I was so scared one of those kids might suspect you and I were, you know…"

"Boyfriends?"

He nodded.

"*Are* we boyfriends?"

Kevin raised a shoulder. "I *think* so."

I rearranged limbs so my elbow rested on the car seat's back and turned toward Kevin. "Boyfriends," I said, "talk to each other more often than once a month."

Kevin looked at me and nodded. "I get that."

"And just because I went water-skiing with my friend didn't give you the right to cut me off. You do stuff with other people all the time and I don't get mad about it."

Kevin turned his gaze back to the windshield. He drew a breath and let it out. Then he returned his gaze to me. "You just watch," he said. "I'm going to treat you better. Every weekend, from now on, I'll spend at least one night with you, sometimes two. And I'll try to remember to call you Thursdays, I promise."

I didn't say anything. I just looked at Kevin and blinked. I wanted to believe he meant what he'd just said. In fact, I suspected he *did*. But that wasn't the problem.

The Kevin I sat next to in the Dart wasn't the Kevin who had shooed me away at the Keating dance; he wasn't the gridiron hero or the guy who could do the Boogaloo and the Mashed Potato like someone on *American Bandstand*. Right now, he was a guy with a cane and a banged-up knee who could barely walk. And I felt pretty certain his calls and visits, if they happened at all, would quickly wane when he recovered from his injury.

Did I really want to give him another chance?

Chapter Fifteen

THE FIRST TUESDAY in December, I sat across from Lane at a Formica-topped cafeteria table. All around us students chattered while they dined on pizza, burgers, or spaghetti with meatballs. The din was so loud we had to raise our voices to hear each other. We both wore sweaters and chinos, and a gold wristwatch gleamed on Lane's wrist.

"Got plans for this weekend?" he asked me in between bites from his burger.

"Why?" I asked.

"The surf's good in Brevard County right now. I was thinking we could drive over there, hit the water, and maybe spend one night."

I nodded while I thought about the powerful waves we'd ridden during our last visit to the east coast. Just thinking about them quickened my pulse. "I have a few yards to mow Saturday, but if I do them in the morning, I could get away right after lunch."

"That works," Lane said. "We can surf an hour or two before dark on Saturday, and then again Sunday morning before we drive back. It'll be fun."

I bobbed my chin, then raised an eyebrow. "Where will we sleep, in your car?"

Lane laughed and shook his head. "I checked my dad's triple-A directory. There's a motel in Cape Canaveral with rooms that go for twenty bucks a night. It won't be as nice as the one we stayed at last time, but who cares? It's just a place to sleep."

"I'm in," I said. "Let's do it."

TWO NIGHTS LATER, only a few minutes past eight, Kevin called me, as he had the previous Thursday. Mom was in our living room watching *The Flying Nun,* a stupid comedy TV series starring Sally Field, so I talked to Kevin on the princess phone in Mom's bedroom.

"How's the knee?" I asked Kevin.

"A little better, but I still have to use the cane. I'm starting to think I'll never fully heal."

I felt slightly guilty because, honestly, I didn't *want* Kevin's knee to get better. As long as he couldn't play football or dance and as long as he hobbled around the hallways of Bishop Keating High, he'd have plenty of time for *me*.

The Corrigans had left town for Thanksgiving weekend to visit relatives who vacationed in Ft. Lauderdale, and then my grandparents from Pennsylvania visited us the following weekend, so I hadn't seen Kevin in over two weeks. Just hearing his voice over the phone made my mouth get sticky.

"I thought I'd spend this weekend at your place," Kevin said. "There's a British band called the Animals; they're playing in Clearwater Saturday night. I can get us tickets if you want."

I fingered the phone's spiral cord while I studied its illuminated rotary dial. "I won't be here Saturday night," I said, then I explained about the trip I'd take with Lane. "But come over Friday," I said, then lowered my voice to a whisper. "My mom's volunteering at the hospital that night, and my sister always babysits on Fridays. We'll have the house to ourselves."

Kevin didn't speak for a few seconds. Then he said, "Is this the same guy you water-skied with?"

"Yeah, why?"

"Are you and he...?"

"I already told you: Lane's just a friend. All we're going to do is surf, so don't be jealous. Now are you coming over Friday or not?"

"I'll come over," Kevin said. "But I'm not happy you're leaving town."

SATURDAY MORNING, AROUND seven, I woke next to Kevin. He lay on his side with his back to me, and I studied the freckles on his shoulders. We had spent time the previous night at a Madeira Beach pool hall, where we smoked L&Ms and played eight ball for two hours or so before returning to my house for a sweet round of sex.

Now, in the chilly morning, I didn't want to leave Kevin, but I dragged my butt from underneath the covers. The morning was cool, so I dressed in a ragged pair of blue jeans and my oldest sweatshirt. I slipped on my beat-up pair of sneakers. Then, after a hasty breakfast, I wheeled my mower and edger to my first job of the day.

Few people stirred in my neighborhood, but my first customers' German shepherd named Duchess greeted me on their driveway. I scratched her behind the ears while my breath steamed in the chilly morning air. Then I cranked up my mower and got busy. I must've worked the job for about a half hour before Kevin drove up to the curb in his Mustang.

I switched off the mower and strode to Kevin's car. I leaned on the passenger door's sill and looked in. "Heading home?" I asked.

Kevin wore the same clothes he had the night before. His hair was tousled and his eyes looked puffy from sleep. His voice croaked when he answered. "No sense in me hanging around your place when you're not there. Guess I'll go home and get back in bed for a while."

I nodded. "I'll call you Sunday night, after I get back from Cocoa Beach."

Kevin crinkled his forehead. "What for?"

"Just to say hi; and to let you know how the surfing went."

He lowered his gaze for a moment, then nodded. I could tell he wasn't at all happy about the trip I was about to take, and I wasn't all that sure he'd care if I called him Sunday night or not. But like always, I assumed he might.

"When your knee gets better," I said, "we'll have to go over to Brevard County, just you and me. I think you'd like it."

Kevin looked at me and tried to smile, but he couldn't manage much more than a grimace. "Have fun," he said and drove away.

LANE PICKED ME up around one p.m. We placed my board atop his on the VW's roof rack, then secured both boards to the rack with a pair of straps. After I tossed my overnight bag onto the backseat, I hung my wetsuit on a hook behind the passenger seat, alongside Lane's. Then we cruised down Gulf Boulevard, heading for the Treasure Island Causeway that would lead us into St. Petersburg. I had just showered and my hair was still damp. I wore jeans and a flannel shirt over a long-sleeved T-shirt. Lane was dressed much the same. His yellow hair fluttered in the breeze while he gripped the steering wheel with his long fingers.

"I've never taken a trip like this without my folks," he said, "and I think it's kind of cool."

I nodded. "I guess this means we're grown-ups, huh?"

Lane grinned while he bobbed his chin. "You should've heard my mom," he said. He spoke in falsetto: "'Drive carefully, especially on the interstate, and don't speed. Be sure to lock your motel room door when you go to bed. And you two eat a decent meal tonight.'"

Then Lane spoke in normal voice, "She even gave me six dollars for our dinners."

The VW's engine chugged while we drove across the Howard Frankland Bridge spanning Tampa Bay. The bay was as calm as a mirror. I saw a pair of dolphin surface for a breath of air. Pelicans bobbed in the placid water while cormorants sunned themselves on the bridge's light poles with their wings spread like war eagles.

We passed downtown Tampa, where several tall buildings created a skyline of sorts, and then took Interstate 4 eastward, toward Orlando. We hurtled past cow pastures, orange groves, and strawberry fields where migrant workers toiled. The road was peppered with billboards advertising tourist attractions like Six Gun Territory and Silver Springs. We passed a Stuckey's Pecan Shoppe offering pecan rolls, saltwater taffy, and hokey tourist souvenirs.

Just before we reached Orlando's outskirts, we exited onto the Beeline Expressway, a two-lane asphalt ribbon that ran due eastward, all the way to the coast. The road bisected cattle ranches and pine forests. Lane and I chattered away about school and certain kids we knew there, about our teachers and our school's lousy football team that had won only two games that fall.

We passed over Interstate 95, and then reached an arching bridge that spanned the Banana River. The bridge connected mainland Florida to Merritt Island where the Kennedy Space Center was located. Off to the north, we saw NASA's rocket assembly building, the one we had toured during our earlier visit, a massive and boxlike structure. Afternoon sunlight glittered in the river's rippling surface while a phalanx of brown pelicans flew beside us in V-formation.

"Have you given any more thought to college?" Lane asked me.

"Not really," I said. "Graduation's still eighteen months away."

Lane looked at me and raised an eyebrow. "You know the SAT's given in April, right?"

I nodded. Already, kids at school were talking about the test and how tough it might be. But I hadn't signed up to take it. You didn't need an SAT score to attend our community college, so why bother?

"My parents bought me an SAT prep book," Lane said. "I have to spend at least three hours a week working on it, no exceptions. They're determined I'll go to Gainesville for school."

I rearranged my limbs while I looked over at Lane. "Is that what *you* want?"

He puckered one side of his face while he rocked his head from side to side. "I don't want to disappoint them, so I *guess* I want to go. It's just that moving away from the coast, and going to school where I don't know anyone, doesn't seem too appealing. Know what I mean?"

I nodded. "Have you been up there to see it?"

"Yeah, my dad took me to a Gator football game back in September. It's a big place—there are 25,000 students—and the dormitories look like prisons."

We came to another arching bridge, this one crossing the Indian River, a much broader expanse of water than the Banana River. At the bridge's apex, we could see the blue Atlantic on the opposite side of the barrier island we approached. A few high-rise hotels lined the ocean's shore.

The time was around three thirty, and shadows had already grown long when we entered Cape Canaveral, a community of cinder-block duplexes, apartment buildings, strip centers, and trailer parks. Our one-story motel faced A-1-A. The motel's crowded parking lot had weeds growing up through cracks in the asphalt, and two spindly palms were the only landscaping. Traffic on the highway roared when we exited the VW.

In the office, an old guy with a face the color of boiled ham stared into the screen of a portable black-and-white TV. A cigarette dangled from his pudgy lower lip. After Lane said he'd reserved a room for one night, the guy checked his registry. Then his gaze flitted between me and Lane.

"You know," he told Lane, "that unit only has one bed."

Lane shrugged; he told the guy, "We'll take it."

The room wasn't much: a queen-size bed with a chenille coverlet, a Formica bureau, a nightstand with a battered table lamp, and a black-and-white TV on a rolling aluminum stand. The ceiling was water-stained and the plaster walls were cracked in here and there. The carpet was worn to the weft in places. The bathroom had a wall sink, a john, and a tiled shower stall with mildewed grout and a plastic curtain.

The whole place smelled like the inside of a shoe.

After we both undressed, we slipped into our wetsuits, then toted our boards across the highway. We were barefooted and the road surface felt cold. We entered Alan Shepard Park, a beachfront facility with picnic shelters, barbecue grills, outdoor showers, and restrooms. Because darkness was nearing, the place was pretty much deserted.

On the beach, Lane and I stood at the Atlantic's edge, staring eastward where a few guys bobbed on their boards about a hundred yards out. A wave appeared behind them, easily waist-height. One surfer turned the nose of his board; he paddled toward shore. The wave lifted him, and then he was on his feet with his arms extended and his knees bent.

Lane looked at me and raised his eyebrows. "Shall we?" he said.

The chilly water turned my hands and feet to ice as we paddled out. An oncoming wave rushed toward us, and we had to capsize our boards to allow the wave to wash over us. I lay submerged, face-up, with my arms wrapped around my board, just listening to the wave's roar. After it passed, we righted ourselves, and recommenced paddling till we reached the other surfers. There were maybe six of us out there. Already, the sun had descended behind taller buildings to the west, and the sky in that direction was a greenish color.

"We've got an hour at best," Lane said. "Let's make the most of it."

We did. Although the waves did not have the power of those we'd surfed during our last visit, they had remarkable longevity. Most rides we caught lasted all the way to the shallows. The air was still, and the only sound was the rumble of waves. As soon as one ride ended for me, I turned the nose of my board eastward, then paddled back out. My wetsuit kept me reasonably warm. I savored the ocean's salty scent and the feel of wind sweeping my cheeks whenever I rode a wave toward shore.

We kept at it until darkness fell and stars began to appear in the eastern horizon. By then my hands and feet were numb and my fingertips looked like prunes. When we returned to the motel, we took turns showering in the cramped bathroom stall. The warm water felt delicious when it pounded my head and achy shoulders. The scents of the motel's soap and shampoo gave me a clean and refreshed feeling.

After I got dressed in my jeans and flannel shirt, I brushed my hair into place before the bathroom's steamy mirror.

When I emerged from the bathroom, Lane watched a football game on our little TV. He was seated on the edge of our bed, and when I sat beside him, he asked me, "Are you as hungry as I am?"

I nodded. All the surfing had burned up my lunch and now my stomach growled.

"Let's cruise the highway," he said. "We'll find someplace good."

Both sides of A-1-A were lined with businesses: motels, restaurants, real estate agencies, bait and tackle shops, and hair salons. Just behind those businesses, on narrow streets perpendicular to the highway, were single-family homes surrounded by twisted live oaks. Night had fallen, and oncoming cars had their headlights illuminated. The air rushing through the car was chilly, so I rolled up my passenger window, and so did Lane.

"Imagine living over here," he said. "You could surf every day."

I nodded. "It feels different from the west coast, doesn't it? The air seems fresher and there's always a breeze, plus there aren't so many old folks. It's not a retirement community."

We found a free-standing Italian restaurant with red-checkered tablecloths and candles stuck into the necks of straw-covered Chianti bottles. Our mustachioed waiter wore a black apron and a warm smile. We followed his recommendation; we ordered lasagna, and it was very good.

By the time we'd returned to our motel, I was yawning. I'd been up since seven, and after all the yard work and surfing I'd done that day, I was tired. When I suggested we call it a night, Lane didn't protest. We took turns brushing our teeth and using the toilet, then climbed under the covers. After Lane extinguished the nightstand lamp, we lay side by side, listening to traffic hum on A-1-A.

"Why don't we get up early tomorrow, right after sunrise?" Lane said. "If there are waves, we can surf a couple of hours and still get back here in time to check out. Sound good?"

"Sure," I said.

I yawned deeply and closed my eyes.

An hour later, when I woke up, I didn't know where I was at first, but then I remembered I was in Cape Canaveral. I lay on my back. The motel room was dark, but a bathroom nightlight offered a bit of illumination, enough so I could see. I blinked a couple of times, then realized why I had wakened.

Lane's hand was inside my briefs.

I stole a glance in his direction. He lay on his side, propped up on an elbow and facing me. I couldn't help myself; right away I stiffened down below, and when I did Lane swung his gaze to me.

"Hey," he said. "Do you mind?"

I swallowed hard. "It's okay."

"You're sure?"

I nodded while my pulse pounded, then I stroked Lane's forearm while his fingers explored the area between my legs.

My thoughts raced as I tried to figure out what was happening. I had never once suspected Lane was gay, or that he felt attracted to me. But now I quickly put the pieces of the puzzle together. For the past three months, Lane had patiently and methodically worked his way into my life. As each week passed, the amount of time we spent together increased steadily, culminating in this road trip, and now, as our bodies came together and his lips traveled over my skin, it occurred to me that Lane had never once mentioned dating a girl. He'd never even *talked* about girls the way most guys our age did, and now I knew it wasn't happenstance that Lane had reserved a room for us with only one bed.

How should I respond?

I let my body make that decision, and my body quickly let me know that Lane was exactly the type of guy I liked. He was beautiful in so many ways. His hair was soft, his skin smooth and warm. His body odor smelled like damp earth, a scent I found arousing. When his tongue dueled with mine and I felt his warm breath on my upper lip, my pulse raced and my heart chugged. What more could I ask for?

When I told him what I wanted most to do, he readily agreed. He took me on my back, and then I felt him thrust inside me while the sunscreen we used as lube made smacking sounds. My orgasm came quickly; it shook me to my core while I shouted nonsense at the ceiling.

After we cleaned ourselves up, we lay in darkness beneath the sheet and blanket while traffic noise filtered in from outside. Lane lay on his back, I on my side with my cheek resting on his sternum.

I listened to his heart beat, then said, "Is this a one-time thing, or do you want something more from me?"

He ran his fingers through my hair. "I want as much as you'll give me."

Aye-yi-yi.

"Things could get tricky," I said, then I explained about Kevin—in detail.

Lane toyed with my ear while he listened. Then he said, "It sounds like this guy uses you whenever he feels like it, and otherwise he ignores you. Don't you think you deserve something better?"

"I probably do," I said, blinking.

Chapter Sixteen

WHEN HE WASN'T shifting gears, Lane held my hand on the drive back to Pinellas County. We didn't talk much, not until I asked Lane when he'd first thought of touching me.

"Take a guess," he said.

"The painting party?"

A smile crossed his lips while he nodded. "I remember when you took your shirt off, and right away, I thought to myself, 'I want this guy. Whatever it takes I'll do.' Then, do you remember when you invited me to surf at the sandbar that first time?"

"Of course."

"We were in your bedroom, changing into our surfing trunks, and when you got naked, I wanted to jump your bones on the spot. Does that surprise you?"

I shook my head while recalling the moment in my room he'd just mentioned, when I had let my gaze travel from Lane's feet to his forehead. I'd tried to memorize every inch of him, especially the bulge of his genitals and the curve of his ass. But I never realized Lane was doing exactly the same thing when he gazed at me. And now that we knew the truth about each other, where did I *want* things to go?

Back in Cape Canaveral, after our Sunday morning surf session, we had showered together in the motel room's mildewed stall, then had sex again, albeit quickly. Afterward, when Lane lay beside me, he brought his lips to my ear.

"I think I'm falling in love with you," he said. "Is that okay?"

A shiver ran through me. "Of course," I said.

But *was* it okay? And what exactly *was* love between two guys, anyway? What would Lane expect from me in the weeks and months ahead? And how easy would it be to hide our relationship from others, especially our families?

As we rolled down I-4 in his VW, Lane was already making plans. "My folks are going on a church retreat, weekend after next. You can spend two nights at my house if you'd like. Sound good?"

I nodded, but I thought about Kevin. He might ask to stay at my place on the same weekend Lane had just mentioned, and how would I explain to Kevin that I'd stay at Lane's instead?

Why were things getting so complicated?

HOURS AFTER LANE dropped me off at home, and right after my sister and I had finished the dinner dishes, I strolled to the phone booth on Gulf Boulevard. Evening traffic whizzed by as I dropped coins into the slots. I dialed the Corrigans' number, then chewed a hangnail while I waited for someone to answer. Finally, on the fifth ring, Kevin's mom picked up.

"He's not here," she said when I asked for Kevin. "He went for a drive."

I glanced at my wristwatch. The time was close to eight. "If he gets home before ten," I said, "will you have him call me?"

But of course Kevin didn't. He didn't call the following Thursday either, and I began to wonder whether he was punishing me for taking the trip to Cape Canaveral. On Friday morning, when I saw Lane in my first-period class, I suggested we visit a drive-in theater movie that night to watch *Casino Royale,* a spoof on the James Bond films that were so popular at the time.

"We can take my car," I said after Lane accepted my invitation. "It's roomier than yours."

Lane waggled his eyebrows in response. "Extra room is always nice," he said.

But when I got home that afternoon, Kevin's car sat in the driveway. Inside, I found him seated on the sofa, next to his overnight bag and cane. He wore his school uniform: khaki slacks, a pique polo shirt with the Bishop Keating crest stitched into it, and his penny loafers. He studied a *Sports Illustrated* issue he must've brought with him, and when he heard me enter, he set the magazine aside.

In the kitchen, my sister emptied an ice tray. I listened to cubes clunk into a glass while I stared at Kevin and crinkled my forehead.

"What are you doing here?" I asked.

He lifted his bag. "What does it look like?"

I glanced toward the kitchen, then jerked a thumb toward our front door. "Let's go outside where we can talk."

When Kevin followed me, I listened to his cane tap our front steps as he slowly descended them. After we leaned against the front fender of Kevin's car, I crossed my arms at my chest.

"You can't stay here tonight," I said. "I have plans."

"Cancel them," Kevin said in a tone that let me know he expected me to do exactly that.

"I can't," I said. "And you shouldn't just show up here expecting to spend the weekend without calling ahead."

Kevin looked at me and raised an eyebrow. "I'm already here, and I'm sure your mom won't mind if I stay over, so what's the problem?"

I hissed. "The problem is you can't just take me for granted, as if I don't have any kind of a life outside of you, because I do. And besides: I called you Sunday night, but you never called me back. And then you didn't call me last night either like you promised you would."

Kevin slapped the sides of his thighs while he shook his head. "I don't believe this. Are you really going to let a couple of missed phone calls keep us from spending the weekend together?"

I kicked sand with my sneaker toe while my thoughts swirled. Kevin, of course, looked like a prince in his school uniform, and the thought I could have him to myself for two days and nights was tempting as hell. He stood close enough to me that I smelled his piney body odor, which, like always, made my pulse quicken. His scent was like liquor to me. I looked at the golden hairs glistening on the back of Kevin's forearm while I rubbed my lips together.

I knew Lane wouldn't get upset if I canceled our date. We had already planned on spending the following weekend together at his house, and if I spent *this* weekend with Kevin, then Kevin wouldn't be able to gripe when I stayed at Lane's for two nights.

I drew a breath, then let it out. "All right, you can stay, but I'll need to make a phone call."

Kevin reached for me and mussed my hair. My scalp prickled when he whispered in my ear.

"You just wait till tonight; you'll be glad you said yes."

SATURDAY AFTERNOON, WHEN I'd finished mowing three lawns, I grabbed a shower. Then I drove Kevin and myself southward to Pass-a-Grille Beach, the first barrier island community ever settled in Pinellas County. Kevin said that a gay bar existed there, and we were curious to see what kind of men might patronize the place. Of course, we couldn't go inside the bar because we were minors, and even if we could've, we wouldn't have. There was no way we'd risk being seen there. But we could park near the bar and watch the comings and goings; we could do at least that.

Pass-a-Grille Way, the island's only access road, was lined with Washingtonia palm trees twenty feet tall. They reminded me of those toothpicks I often saw at parties, the kind with crinkles of cellophane at one end. Homes we passed were a mixture of older cottages and contemporary cinder-block houses with tile roofs. Lawns were well-tended and a variety of flowering shrubs gave the place a tropical look.

The day was sunny and breezy. We both wore sweaters, corduroy jeans, and sneakers. Cool wind rushed through the Dart's open windows. A local radio played the song, "GTO," by Ronny & the Daytonas, but I wasn't paying attention to it. My thoughts dwelt on the night before, when Kevin and I were alone at my house. My sister was at a movie with friends and my mom was volunteering at the kids' hospital. As soon as my sister left for the movie, Kevin grabbed my hand. He led me into my room, where he pushed me onto the bed. Then he peeled my clothes off while making slutty remarks about what lay in store for me.

Once I was naked, Kevin told me to undress *him*, which I was more than happy to do. After I finished the task, Kevin climbed on top of me. Because he hadn't showered since that morning, his body odor seemed stronger than normal, and his scent got me all excited. By the time we'd finished our session, I was short of breath and my sheets were damp. The two of us lay on our backs with our chests rising and falling while a breeze stirred the venetian blinds, and I told myself, *That was unbelievable.*

But now, in my car on Pass-a-Grille Way, I asked myself for the tenth time if I'd made a mistake by letting Kevin stay with me for the weekend. When I'd called Lane to cancel our movie date, I could tell he was disappointed. I told him a complete lie: that a family situation had come up that required me to stay home, and he accepted my explanation without complaint, which only made me feel guiltier.

Now, on Pass-a-Grille Beach, Kevin and I arrived at the street where the gay bar was located. The place was called Jack's; it occupied one quarter of a city block. The one-story building was nondescript and looked like it hadn't been painted in twenty years. Its wooden sign was no bigger than the Dart's windshield. After I street-parked in a space maybe thirty yards from Jack's, Kevin and I lit up two L&Ms from a pack we'd purchased a half hour before. Our parking space afforded us a clear view of the bar's front door.

I'm not sure what I'd expected to see, but as men came and went from Jack's, the first thing I noticed was how *normal* they appeared. They didn't wear garish clothing or sport weird hairstyles. Instead each guy looked like he might be a postman or a school teacher or a barber. Two guys who looked about thirty-five left the bar together. They both wore chinos, button-down paisley shirts, and penny loafers. One guy smoked a cigarette. When they strolled past us on the sidewalk, they discussed the most mundane of topics: which restaurant they would dine at that evening.

"I wonder what goes on *inside* Jack's?" Kevin said after the couple passed us by. "Do you think there's dancing, or is it just a place to drink and meet guys?"

"Beats me," I said, as I tried to imagine Kevin and me dancing together in Jack's, in front of all the other patrons. Then it occurred to me that Kevin and I had *never* once danced together, not fast or slow, even though we'd had plenty of opportunities to do so at my house, and I wondered what he might say if I asked him to.

Kevin jerked a thumb over his shoulder, in the direction the gay couple had gone. "Do you think those two guys live together?"

I lit a fresh L&M, then blew a stream of smoke out my driver's window. "I'll bet they do, and I wonder what their neighbors think about it."

Kevin shrugged. Then he turned to me and said, "Remember when I said you and I could move to another city and live together like that?"

I nodded.

"I still think about it sometimes," Kevin said. "Do you ever?"

I stuck my arm out the window to tap my ash, then looked at Kevin. "Not really," I said. "In fact, I don't think us living together is a realistic idea."

Kevin gathered his eyebrows. "Why not?"

I rolled my eyes. "We've talked about this *way* too many times. You're not the kind of guy who can make a commitment and stick to it. Hell, you can't even call me at a certain time once a week, so how could you possibly live with me and keep up your end of things?"

"What kind of things?"

"I don't know...like coming home when you say you will, or helping pay the bills or cleaning the bathroom. I can't see you scrubbing a toilet, and I sure don't see you being faithful to me either. For all I know, you're still screwing that neighbor of yours when you're not screwing me."

Kevin hissed. "I haven't seen that guy in months."

After I turned to Kevin, I put my arm on the seatback. "Back in October, when I went water-skiing with my friend Lane, do you remember how mad you got at me?"

Kevin nodded.

"I tried calling you that night, when I got home, but your mom told me you weren't there. She said you were visiting a neighbor, so why don't you tell me *which* neighbor it was?"

Kevin lowered his gaze. Then he grimaced and shook his head. "You sound like a jealous bitch, do you know that?"

I crossed my arms at my chest while anger boiled in my belly. I wasn't backing down on this one. "You still haven't answered my question," I said. "Which neighbor was it?"

"What does it matter?"

"It matters a lot if we're going to be boyfriends."

Kevin reached for the L&M pack, and after he lit a cigarette, he slouched in the car seat, just smoking and staring out the windshield at the Jack's entrance. I followed suit, and neither of us said a word for at least five minutes, not until a pair of guys, maybe thirty or so, emerged from the bar. They stood on the sidewalk in front of Jack's. One guy's face was red and his expression was distorted. He seemed to spit out words at the other guy while waving his hands here and there. The other guy stood on the sidewalk with his hands in the rear pockets of his chinos. He kept his chin lowered and his gaze fixed on the sidewalk.

Kevin blew air out his nose. "I'll bet that's what *we* look like when we fight."

I tossed my cigarette, then rearranged my limbs. "We wouldn't *have* to fight if you'd show a little respect for me. Why is that so hard for you to do?"

Kevin didn't answer me; he only shrugged.

SATURDAY NIGHT, KEVIN drove us to downtown St. Petersburg, where a rock band played for free at the band shell at Williams Park, a rectangle of greenspace with towering live oaks, azalea shrubs, and plenty of benches arranged in a semicircle around the stage. The band was from Tampa; they were fairly talented, especially the singer and the lead guitar player. They played numbers by the Jefferson Airplane, Buffalo Springfield, Jimi Hendrix, the Yardbirds, and the Doors.

Some of the guys in the audience had grown their hair past their shoulders; they wore dashiki shirts, bell-bottomed blue jeans, headbands, and sandals. A thick cloud of smoke hung over the crowd, and the odor of burning marijuana was strong.

I, of course, had never smoked grass at that point in my life. In fact, I didn't even know anyone who had. But as I watched a long-haired guy and his girlfriend share a joint, I wondered exactly how the stuff might make you feel. The couple I watched grinned at each other from time to time, but they weren't acting weird at all.

On the way home, while we sat at a traffic light, I asked Kevin, "Would you ever consider smoking grass?"

He shrugged. "Maybe. I know a few guys at school who smoke; I could get us some if you'd like to try it. The stuff's not all that expensive."

"We might be missing out on something," I said. "Maybe sometime soon we should smoke a joint, just to see what it's like."

By the time we reached home, the time was eleven thirty. My mom had already turned in, but my sister was watching the tail end of Alfred Hitchcock's film *Psycho* on TV. We watched the rest with her, and I really liked the scene when Norman Bates, dressed as his mother, stabs the private detective on the staircase. Then it was time for bed.

Kevin and I always slept naked now; we kept my bedroom door locked so our privacy wouldn't be intruded upon, and after we crawled between the covers, we lay side by side on our backs, just staring at the ceiling while the occasional car roared past on Gulf Boulevard.

"What do you feel like doing?" Kevin asked.

The concert and what I'd seen there had stirred something inside me. Was it curiosity?

"Something different," I said.

"I have an idea," Kevin said, then made a suggestion that took me completely by surprise. "Would you like to try screwing me for a change?"

What?

His question made my head spin. After all, our roles in bed had always been clearly defined, ever since the inception of our sexual relationship, and now the thought I'd be top man for a night had my heart racing. After a half hour of foreplay, I brought out the jelly and hand towels. Then we took our positions on the sheet. Kevin lay face-up with the backs of his knees resting on my shoulders while I knelt before him. His legs were a bit heavy, but I didn't mind; my body tingled all over.

Kevin held my hip while he guided me inside him. "Easy," he whispered as I felt him stretch. "This isn't something I'm used to."

I had never penetrated another guy before, and now I knew why both Kevin and Lane craved this sort of surrender from me. The warmth of Kevin's gut felt amazing. When I commenced thrusting, Kevin grunted each time my hips smacked his ass, and it didn't take more than five minutes before we both reached orgasm. I cried out when it happened— I couldn't help myself—and collapsed onto Kevin, feeling satisfied in a way I'd never really known before.

"That was...beyond great," I whispered after I finally caught my breath.

Kevin ran his fingers through my hair. "You liked it?"

"Heck, yeah."

After we separated, we went about cleaning ourselves, and then I asked Kevin a question. "Tell me something: did *you* like what we just did?"

Kevin raised a shoulder. "It hurt a little at first, but once I relaxed, it felt really good. And look, I shouldn't always be the guy on top."

His words made my heart sing—his statement was totally out of character for Kevin—and once again, I asked myself if perhaps we'd turned a corner, maybe due to the conversation we'd held in my car outside of Jack's. Was it possible Kevin had finally decided to recognize me as his equal?

We slept with Kevin's cheek resting on my sternum and his arm draping my belly. His warm breath swept my ribs, and he quickly fell asleep, leaving me to my own thoughts. At that point, there was no doubt in my mind I'd made the right decision by letting Kevin stay the weekend. Otherwise, what we'd just done would never have happened. Would Kevin let me do it again one day?

I also thought about Lane and where my budding relationship with him might be headed. How serious did I want it to become, and could I possibly juggle a life with two boyfriends in it?

Chapter Seventeen

SUNDAY AFTERNOON, NOT long after Kevin left for Largo, Lane phoned me, and just hearing his voice took me back to the Cape Canaveral motel and what we had done there.

"My VW broke down yesterday," he said. "It's in the shop—for how long I don't know. Could you give me a lift to school tomorrow?"

"Sure," I said. "It's not a problem," and then we talked about our upcoming weekend.

"If the weather's good," Lane said, "we should take my family's boat to Egmont Key. Ever been there?"

"Never," I said. "What is it?"

"An island near the mouth of Tampa Bay. It's a very cool place with a lighthouse and an old fort we can explore. What do you say?"

"Sounds great," I said, but already I felt guilty about spending an entire weekend with Lane when I knew Kevin would want to be with me. The night before, Kevin had submitted to me in a significant manner. I believed he had told me, in his own way, that I owned him just like he owned me. So would I seem like an ingrate if I left him alone next weekend?

At the same time, I really looked forward to Friday night. Lane and I would have his house to ourselves, and not just for a few hours, but for two whole days and nights. I could only imagine the mischief we'd get into, and just thinking about it made me shiver.

"I'll pick you up at seven fifteen," I told Lane.

"Great," he said. "I'll be ready."

THE WEEK RACED by.

Lane's car needed a serious repair—it was something having to do with the transmission—so he rode to and from school with me every day.

And while we didn't do much other than discreetly hold hands, it felt great being with him so often.

Because I would spend all weekend at Lane's, I altered my lawn care schedule so I could service all my customers between Monday and Thursday. And since darkness falls early in December, I had to work quickly, knocking out two lawns per day, right after school, which made for an exhausting schedule. On Thursday afternoon, just after sunset, I rolled my mower and edger homeward, savoring the cool evening air and thinking about something Lane had told me when I dropped him off after school that day.

"There are special things I want to do with you tomorrow night, so I hope you're ready for some fun." He winked at me while a shiver ran through my limbs.

Now, after I stowed the mower and edger in our garage, I took a warm shower, then spent a half hour at our kitchen table, talking with my mom while she peeled and sliced potatoes. She, of course, already knew where I'd spend the upcoming weekend, and when I mentioned a possible visit to Egmont Key, she sighed and shook her head.

"I went there with a group of kids when I was in high school," she said. "You'll love the island—it's such a pretty place—but what about Kevin?"

"What about him?"

She glanced at me briefly before returning her gaze to her work. "Last weekend, you boys seemed inseparable. So what'll Kevin do without you *this* weekend?"

My scalp prickled at Mom's remark, and again I found myself wondering if she knew what went on in my bedroom whenever Kevin slept over. "Kevin will be okay," I said. "He'll find something else to do."

But Kevin *wasn't* okay when he and I talked two hours later. He phoned at exactly eight p.m. I took the call in my mom's bedroom, and when I told Kevin of my plans with Lane, he exploded.

"You're spending the whole weekend with this guy? What about us?"

"It's just two days," I said. "And besides, I spent last weekend with you; I even canceled my other plans so we could be together."

Over the phone line, I heard a loud bang, as if Kevin had kicked over a trashcan or a chair. "At least let me come over Friday night," Kevin said. "I'll go home Saturday morning, and then you can do whatever you want to with your *pal*, if that's all he really is."

I drew a breath, then let it out while I twirled the phone cord around my finger. Once again, Kevin was insisting I alter my plans with Lane, and again I had a choice to make. I had already canceled on Lane once and didn't want to do it again, but Kevin's neediness gnawed at me. What should I do?

"Listen," I said. "Why don't you come over here tonight? We can take a drive in my car; we'll find someplace private where—"

"Is that the best you can do?" Kevin cried.

"You aren't being fair," I said. "I'm entitled to make plans with other people; it's not like you and I are married."

"Fine," Kevin said. "I guess what I gave you Saturday night didn't mean that much to you. So, go ahead, have a great time. I'll just sit here at home with my dick in my hand."

Before I could say anything in response, Kevin slammed down his receiver. I sat there listening to my phone's dial tone while I stared at the carpet and wondered where all this would lead to.

DURING MY SIXTH-PERIOD class on Friday, I squirmed in my seat like a kid waiting to board a carnival ride. I kept glancing at the classroom clock, but the clock's hands barely seemed to move. My English Lit teacher talked about a scene in William Faulkner's novel *The Sound and the Fury*, but I couldn't concentrate on what she said.

All I could think of was Lane.

On our drive to school that morning, while I steered the Dart down First Avenue South, Lane's hand traveled from my knee to my groin. He squeezed my tender flesh, then said, "I can't wait to get you back to my place." I got so stiff I had to wait ten minutes in the Dart once we reached school just for my erection to subside before I went to class. I barely beat the first-period tardy bell.

Now I leaned against the Dart's front fender in my school's parking lot, smoking a cigarette while kids teemed past me, heading for their cars and chattering about their weekend plans: seeing a movie, going to a party, or whatever. But I was pretty sure none of them had plans like Lane and I did.

The afternoon sun burned in a cloudless sky. The air was chilly; I wore jeans along with a sweater layered over a button-down Oxford-cloth shirt, and yet still I shivered when a wind gust ruffled my hair. I watched Lane approach with his fluid gait. His yellow hair fluttered about his face and shoulders. He carried a notebook and two texts under an arm; they rode on his hip. When he drew near me, his gaze locked onto mine, and a sexy grin crossed his lips.

A tremble started in my feet; it worked its way up my legs and into my torso. It found its way into my fingers even, and when Lane said hi, my voice cracked like a seventh grader's when I said hi back.

Lane crinkled his forehead while he studied my face. "You're looking a bit pale. Are you okay?"

I lowered my gaze and licked my lips. Then I looked at Lane again. "I guess I'm a little nervous," I said. "But in a good way."

He smiled, then nodded. "I'm a little nervous too. This isn't going to be like Cape Canaveral. We'll have the whole weekend to ourselves, with no interruptions. And we'll have a house, a boat, and your car. We can do anything we want to, can't we?"

I nodded while I told myself, *This will be unlike anything I've done before.*

When we got to Lane's, he let us in with a key. I followed him to his bedroom, where I tossed my overnight bag into a corner. The room was carpeted, with a queen-size bed, a bureau with a mirror, and a walk-in closet. Lane even had his own bathroom with a toilet, sink, and tiled shower. The room's windows offered views of Boca Ciega Bay and the Davises' shiny powerboat that hung from their dock davits. The boat looked like a freshly scrubbed tooth.

Afternoon sunlight slanted into the room; the light gave objects a burnished look. Lane wrapped an arm around my waist. After he placed his hand on the back of my neck, he pulled me to him. His mouth met mine, and our tongues dueled while I smelled Lane's earthy body odor. Our lip-smacking was the only sound in the room. I ran my fingers through Lane's hair while we slobbered. Our hips pressed together, and I felt Lane's erection nudge mine.

I won't go into detail about everything that happened during the next hour, but Lane introduced me to a few practices Kevin and I had never shared, including something Lane called "rimming." It drove me nuts because the feel of his tongue exploring the cleft of my ass felt so good. We also got a little kinky. At Lane's request, I let him tie my hands to the headboard and blindfold me. I lay face-up on his bed, unable to see, but quite able to feel Lane's tongue travel over my body.

Early on, he sucked and gently chewed on a spot near my collarbone; it was the first time I'd ever received a hickey, and after he finished his work, Lane continued moving southward. He took his time, and by the time he tongued my navel, I was squirming with pleasure on the mattress. He even sucked my toes, which felt pretty damned incredible.

When Lane finally released me and removed the blindfold, I was a tiger ready to pounce. "I'm on top this afternoon," I told him, "unless you have a problem with that."

Lane shook his head while his eyes glittered. I took him on his back, just as I'd done with Kevin the weekend before. When I entered him, a blue vein popped up on Lane's forehead; he sucked air through his clenched teeth.

"Am I hurting you?" I asked.

"Nope," he said. "I can take it."

I didn't rush things. I kept up a slow and steady cadence with my hips. The bedsprings moaned and the headboard knocked on the wall as I thrust. Lane grunted while he stared into my eyes and chewed his lips. I felt his hot breath on my chest each time he exhaled. After ten minutes or so, Lane reached orgasm, and then I came inside him only moments later. Like my last time with Kevin, I felt my orgasm in every part of my body, even in the soles of my feet. When I closed my eyes, I saw fireworks. I cried out Lane's name and the sound of my voice echoed off the walls.

After I collapsed on top of Lane, I gasped for air while our sweaty skins stuck together like they'd been glued. I stayed inside him for several minutes while our pulses slowed. We didn't say anything; we just listened to each other breathe. The scent of our sex was strong in the room. When I finally pulled out, we lay side by side on the bed, just staring at the plaster ceiling and holding each other's hands.

"I knew this would be good," Lane said, "but not *that* good. The whole thing was *so* much better than sex at the motel."

I nodded while Lane turned onto his side, facing me. He bent an elbow and rested his chin on his palm. "Who's on top when you're with Kevin?"

I explained about my role reversal with Kevin the previous weekend. "I mean, I always enjoyed being on the bottom before—I never once complained about it—but there's something amazing about poking another guy, isn't there?"

Lane nodded. "We can mix it up this weekend; how's that?"

After we showered, we hit the kitchen, wearing nothing but our briefs. Both of us were famished after all the energy we'd burned in Lane's bedroom. His mom had left us a fridge full of sodas and a pantry stocked with snacks, the kind of junk food guys our age craved: potato chips, cheese doodles, pretzels, and cookies. We sat at the kitchen table and munched away like we hadn't eaten in a week.

"How long have you known you were gay?" I asked Lane in between munches.

He snickered. "Ever since my cousin from Virginia slept in my room, two summers ago. He's a horny guy—he's a bit kinky too—and not at all bashful. He got inside my briefs the very first night, and right away, I knew I liked it. Girls have never interested me; how about you?"

I shook my head. "I've never even gone on a *date* with a girl, and why would I? I just never felt the urge. I figured I'd go through life alone, but when Kevin and I had sex the first time, it was like he'd let me out of a cage. After that, I couldn't get enough of him."

"Does your mom know?" Lane asked.

I shrugged. "I think she might suspect, but she hasn't said anything—not yet."

Lane studied a pretzel while he talked. "Back in July, I told my folks. They bugged me so much about why I wasn't dating, and finally I got tired of making excuses. I said to them, 'There's something you need to understand: I'm not attracted to girls, and you know what *that* means.'"

I whistled. "How'd they react?"

Lane shrugged. "They were shocked, of course. They thought maybe I needed counseling, but I told them I didn't. I said I didn't want to pretend I was someone I wasn't, and I think they respected my honesty."

I nodded and tried to imagine having such a conversation with *my* mom and sister. What if I told them about Kevin and me? Would Mom let Kevin spend the night anymore?

"Let's get dressed," Lane said. "I need to turn on the outdoor Christmas lights."

Because it was chilly outside, Lane loaned me a leather bomber-style jacket to wear over my sweater, and then we walked around the perimeter of his house, plugging in light strands that covered the hedges and circled the trunks of palms. Extension cords snaked everywhere. We plugged in an illuminated Santa that stood on the Davises' roof, and then we plugged in more light strands decorating their dock. By the time we'd finished our work, the property looked like a Christmas parade float.

Lane snitched two cans of beer from a fridge in his garage, and we sat on the dock, admiring all the lights. Their glow reflected in Lane's hair, in his wheat-colored eyelashes and his gray eyes. After he glanced here and there, he took my hand in his and kissed my cheek.

"You're such a sweet guy," he told me. "I'm glad you could stay here this weekend."

"Me too," I said. And then, between sips of beer, I told Lane about my phone conversation with Kevin the night before. "It's like he thinks he owns me."

Lane shook his head. "I don't understand why you put up with it."

"It's hard to explain. I mean, Kevin and I go back a long way. I know him better than anyone else does. His home life is pretty dismal; I'm all he has to lean on when times get tough. And also..."

"What?"

"He's sexy as hell."

I reached for my wallet and showed Lane a school photo of Kevin that Kevin had recently given me, a black-and-white headshot with Kevin dressed in a jacket and tie. Lane studied the photo for a few moments while he rubbed his lips together. Then he handed it back to me.

"He *is* good-looking, but that doesn't mean he should treat you like he does."

"You're right," I said, then realized I was already tired of thinking about Kevin and how often he neglected me. "Why don't we talk about something else?"

"Okay," he said. "Come back inside with me; I have a surprise for you."

I crinkled my forehead while I drained the last of my beer. Already I felt a little light-headed from the alcohol. "What kind of surprise?"

After Lane rose, he held out his hand. "Come on." He pulled me to my feet. "I'll show you."

Back in Lane's room, where the scent of our sex still hung in the air, Lane produced a gift-wrapped rectangular package from his closet. After he handed it to me, we sat side by side on his bed, and I placed the package in my lap.

"Go on," Lane said. "Open it."

I untied the bow and ripped the brightly colored paper apart. The gift was an SAT preparation guide, a book almost four inches thick.

"My folks bought it for you," Lane said.

"I don't understand. Why?"

Lane mussed my hair. "'Cause they think you're university material, that's why. You still have more than three months to get ready for the test."

I leafed through the guide while savoring its new book smell. The guide's first half was dedicated the test's verbal portion while the second half was devoted to math. In the rear were four practice exams.

"It's a lot of work," I said.

Lane nodded. "Take it in bite-size chunks, a couple of hours at a time. That's how I'm doing it, and you'd be surprised how quickly you can progress through the pages."

I didn't know what to say. No one outside of my mom and sister had ever given me a gift, and certainly not something substantial like this book. I felt so overwhelmed my eyes itched and I had to clear my throat before I spoke.

"This was really nice of your parents," I said. "I'll be sure to send them a thank-you note."

Lane put an arm around my shoulders and gave me a squeeze. "They like you," he said. "They know how hard you work on your lawn business and how well you perform in school. They want to see you succeed."

I looked at Lane and raised an eyebrow. "Do you think they suspect you and I...?"

Lane shrugged.

Then I asked, "Do they even know I'm here this weekend?"

"Of course," Lane said. "I don't like to hide things from them."

An hour later, we devoured burgers and fries at a Treasure Island A&W drive-in restaurant where two dozen kids from our school were hanging out. Radios played in cars while two waitresses delivered food on trays. We saw a few kids we both knew; we waved hello, and I felt very proud to be seen in Lane's company. Glow from the drive-in's neon lights reflected in the Dart's shiny hood while I sipped from a soda cup.

Lane dipped a french fry in a little container of ketchup on the dashboard. Then he asked me, "What do you think all these kids would say if they knew our story?"

I raised my eyebrows while I shifted my buttocks in the car seat. "To be honest, I wouldn't want to find out. I think we'll have to be very careful when we're out in public together, don't you agree?"

Lane nodded, and I told him how Kevin had suggested, more than once, that he and I live together after we finished high school. "He thinks we should move to New York where people don't care if you're gay."

Lane looked at me and raised his eyebrows. "Would you actually consider doing that?"

"You mean with Kevin?"

When Lane nodded again, I made a face. "Probably not," I said. "He isn't reliable; I can't count on him to do what he says he will."

"But how about with someone else, a guy you *could* trust?"

I stared out the windshield and blinked. "Maybe."

WE SLEPT SPOON-STYLE in Lane's bed Friday night. I fell asleep very quickly with my back to Lane and his arm wrapped around my waist. When I woke Saturday morning, bright sunlight poured through the windows. We had changed positions during the night, and now Lane lay on his back with his cheek resting against my shoulder. I studied his facial features: his eyebrows and eyelashes, and his pink lips; they each seemed as delicate as flower petals. Sunlight reflected in the golden stubble on his chin. I kissed his forehead and buried the tip of my nose in his hair.

Lane's eyelids fluttered open. When he looked at me, a little smile crossed his lips. He stretched his limbs like a housecat, then asked me, "How'd you sleep?"

"Great," I said.

We both peed into Lane's toilet at the same time—I found it kind of sexy—and after we flushed, we returned to the bed. We crawled under the covers, and our bodies intertwined while our lips smacked and our tongues rubbed.

This time Lane took me on my back, and because we were alone in the house, we both uttered some pretty lewd remarks while Lane thrust inside me and the bedsprings sang. I think Lane called me his "fuckboy" at one point, which I also thought was kind of sexy. I felt like I was riding a rocket hurtling into space, and when I hit orgasm, my vision blurred.

Lane's entire body jerked three or four times when he unloaded inside me. After our heartbeats slowed, we lay side by side on our backs, both of us with our fingers interlaced behind our necks. Our shoulders and hips touched and our leg hairs commingled.

Lane glanced out the windows. "It's a sunny day," he said, "and the wind's not blowing, so I think Egmont Key's doable. We'll just have to bundle up 'cause it'll be cold on the water when the engine runs full-throttle."

We showered together. I soaped and scrubbed Lane with a washcloth, and he did the same to me. We both washed our hair too. After we toweled off, we ate our breakfast at the kitchen table, butt naked. Lane looked so sexy with his damp hair and his sleek muscles that I couldn't help myself; I kept pawing his limbs in between spoonfuls of Cheerios.

Lane took one of my hands in his. He slipped his fingers in between mine and squeezed. "This is so cool," he said. "Why can't it be like this all the time?"

I lowered my gaze and made a little smile.

Yeah, I thought, *why can't it?*

Chapter Eighteen

I SUPPOSE EVERY guy experiences at least one special day in his life that he carries deep in his heart forever. My Saturday with Lane was one of those. I remember everything about it: the sights, the sounds, and the scents. I will always remember the way Lane looked when he stood at his boat's helm with the wind fluttering his hair and sunlight dancing on the surface of Boca Ciega Bay.

We departed around ten a.m. with an ice cooler holding sodas and sandwiches. We both wore jeans, sweatshirts, and jackets. The day was cool and sunny, and because the breeze was light, water in the bay wasn't choppy. The boat's hull plowed the placid water like a knife slicing whipped butter while chilly air burned my cheeks.

I stood alongside Lane, watching him adjust the engine's speed and tilt. He explained the function of the red and green channel markers we passed, and how they kept boats from running aground. We passed by waterfront communities where low-slung homes stood behind seawalls. Many homes had docks with sailboats bobbing alongside them or powerboats hanging from davits. We passed under a drawbridge connecting St. Pete Beach to South Pasadena, an imposing concrete-and-steel structure that made me feel a little bit vulnerable in our little boat.

Lane pointed westward, toward more waterfront neighborhoods that looked pretty much like the ones we'd already passed. "That's Three Palms Point, and then the next one is Brightwater; they're dredge-and-fill islands that weren't there twenty years ago. My dad says all that dredging really screwed up fishing in the area. They tore up the sea grasses where fish used to spawn, and now you can cast here all day without catching a thing."

After we left the dredge-and-fill islands behind us, the homes we passed began to look older, the streets narrower, and I realized we had reached Pass-a-Grille Beach. I thought about the Saturday before, when

Kevin and had I parked outside of Jack's, and then I thought about the squabble we had after Kevin suggested, for a second time, how we might live together one day. I remembered how Kevin said I was acting like a "jealous bitch" when I complained of his neglect, and now the memory of that moment stirred anger in my belly.

The more time I spent with Lane, the less guilty I felt about not spending time with Kevin that weekend. At least Lane had never called me a bitch, nor had he taken our friendship for granted the way Kevin had. Lane treated me like an equal, even though he came from circumstances far more prosperous than mine, and I liked that.

We entered the Gulf of Mexico via the Pass-a-Grille Channel. Lane took us about a mile offshore before turning the bow southward. We navigated in deep water now, and the boat's hull rose and fell with the swells we encountered. It seemed like we occupied an elevator car that kept going back and forth between floors. I felt uneasy about the whole situation; I wondered if perhaps I should put on a life jacket, but I tried to stay calm. I didn't want Lane to think I was a wimp.

When the Gulf's color changed from emerald to midnight blue, Lane told me, "We're entering the shipping channel; it leads to the Sunshine Skyway Bridge and then to Tampa Bay. The depth here is about eighty feet."

Eighty feet? My stomach did a flip-flop while I seized a grab bar on the console with both my hands. Off in the distance, a hulking freighter approached; it looked like a floating warehouse plowing through the water.

"Are you sure it's safe to be out here?" I asked Lane, and pointed at the freighter. "Our boat's not big like that one and—"

Lane put his hand on the back of my neck. Then he squeezed. "Relax, Jesse. You know I'd never put you in danger."

Right away, Lane's touch and the sound of his voice calmed me. I relaxed my grip on the grab bar, then bent my knees so my body could bob with the roll of the swells we encountered. Up ahead, another island loomed, this one with a lighthouse towering above a forest of Sabal palms.

"That's Egmont," Lane said while pointing with his chin. "We'll dock on the lee side and then go ashore."

I drew a breath, then let it out. The idea of walking onto dry land seemed like a dream I couldn't wait to come true. Lane steered the boat in a southeasterly direction until we passed Egmont's northernmost point, and I saw a concrete dock with two boats tethered to it. As soon as we drew east of the island, the swells disappeared. The water flattened out, and as Lane throttled down, I saw the bay's sandy bottom as we puttered toward the dock.

I raised my chin and gazed into the cloudless sky.

Hallelujah. We actually made it...

Lane tossed an anchor off the stern of the boat, then ambled toward the bow just as we reached the dock. He seized a bow line and leapt like a gazelle from the bow to the dock. After he tied the line to a cleat on the dock, he told me to come ashore. I felt a little awkward getting off the boat, but I managed to hop onto the dock, then I savored the solid feel of the concrete deck.

Lane glanced at his wristwatch. "It's eleven right now. Let's explore for an hour, and then we'll have ourselves some lunch. Sound good?"

I nodded and followed Lane up a sandy path that led to a clearing where the lighthouse and a group of small one-story buildings stood. The buildings didn't appear to be in use. While we made our way up the path, we encountered a turtle as large as a Thanksgiving turkey; it was chewing flowers off a ground vine, and it didn't seem the least intimidated by our presence.

"That's a gopher tortoise," Lane said. "Much of the time, they live underground in tunnels they create. They can live for sixty years because they don't have any natural enemies, other than man of course."

When we reached the lighthouse, Lane said, "We can't go inside; they keep the door locked."

I was fine with that. My stomach still felt queasy after our boat ride, and I didn't feel like climbing a lot of stairs right then. We visored our eyes with our hands to watch a cylindrical light fixture at the tower's apex slowly rotate.

Lane said, "There used to be an old-style lantern inside a glass box up there, but then they finally replaced it with an aerobeacon that doesn't require constant tending. Now no one lives out here."

I looked around me. Aside from the clearing we stood in, the rest of the island seemed to be forested. Lane led us to a brick road maybe twenty feet wide, lined on either side by Sabal palms, and we strolled down the road while Lane talked.

"You have to understand, at one time nearly two hundred men were stationed out here at Fort Dade. It was like a small town, with a movie theater, a mess hall, and barracks. A lighthouse keeper lived out here with his family too. Trucks and horse-drawn wagons used these roads to haul stuff to and from the dock."

The day was warming up, and we both stopped to remove our jackets. After we slung the jackets over our shoulders, Lane took my hand in his. "There's hardly anyone out here today," he said. "I think we're safe to walk like this for a while."

The road branched off here and there, with the side roads leading to abandoned cinder-block structures of varying sizes. Most of the structures had lost their roofs and windows; they looked forlorn and lonely, and it was hard for me to imagine the island as a beehive of military activity.

The remains of Fort Dade sat on the island's northwest corner. Built mostly of poured concrete, it too had a forlorn look to it, as if the structure knew its usefulness had long since passed. But the views from atop the fort's ramparts were spectacular. We could see Ft. De Soto on the other side of the channel we'd earlier crossed. The water on the island's western shore was emerald in color. Two families with small children picnicked on the beach below us where the sand was as white as table sugar.

We wound our way back toward the boat, passing through a junglelike forest of trees I didn't recognize. Again, Lane took my hand in his. Then, when we came to a dark and secluded spot, he pulled me to him. We dropped our jackets onto the bricks. Our lips came together. I explored Lane's mouth with my tongue while he squeezed my butt cheeks through the seat of my jeans.

Lane pulled his mouth from mine. He looked into my eyes, and then said, "I've always liked it out here, but never so much as now. Having you with me makes it special, know what I mean?"

I nodded while a shiver ran through me.

Twenty minutes later, we shared our lunch at a picnic table in a shaded area near the lighthouse clearing. A breeze tickled fronds on nearby Sabal palms while we dined on our ham and cheese sandwiches and slurped from soda bottles.

"Is there anything special you'd like to do tonight?" Lane asked me. "Other than, you know..."

I lowered my gaze to the tabletop, then returned my gaze to Lane's. "I have the money I earned this week tending yards. I want to take you out to dinner, someplace decent. How about it?"

"Sure," Lane said. "We've never gone on a date before, have we?"

"No," I said, "and it's about time we did, don't you think?"

He nodded. "Does Kevin ever take you out places?"

I pursed my lips and shook my head. Then I told Lane about the time I'd gone in search of Kevin at the Keating High School dance and how Kevin behaved when I found him. "He made something clear that night: his time spent with me is something he'll always keep separate from the rest of his life."

Lane made a face. "It almost sounds like he's ashamed of what he shares with you."

"Yeah, I think he is."

"Are *you* ashamed?"

I shook my head.

Lane looked left and right, then stroked my cheek with a fingertip. "You're beautiful, Jesse. No guy should ever feel embarrassed about what he does privately with you."

I lowered my gaze while a lump formed in my throat. Lane, I knew, was right. From the beginning of my sexual relationship with Kevin, he had always treated me like a dirty secret he didn't want to share with anyone. He'd never told me I was attractive, and more than once, he'd cut off seeing me as easily as turning off a water tap.

Didn't I deserve something better?

Hours later, after we'd returned to Lane's and hung the boat from the Davises' dock davits, we spent an hour in Lane's bedroom, getting lusty. We took a lazy shower together afterward, and then Lane loaned me a long-sleeved shirt with his initials stitched onto the breast pocket. I wore it with a pair of chinos I'd packed in my bag. Lane dressed pretty much the same way, and aside from our long hair, we must've looked like two prep school boys.

The sun had already set and the temperature was plunging while we turned on all the Davises' outdoor Christmas lights. I wore the jacket Lane had loaned me the day before to ward off the cold; it was the same jacket I'd worn on the trip to Egmont Key, and in a way, I felt like the jacket belonged to me now. I liked it and wondered if maybe Lane would sell it to me if I asked.

I took us in the Dart to the Kingfish Restaurant at John's Pass, not far from where I often fished. The place was packed when we arrived, and we had to wait fifteen minutes or so before we got a table. The restaurant's walls were paneled in shellacked knotty pine. Several taxidermic fish hung on them, including a tarpon nearly six feet long with a glass eye that seemed to stare at me. Lawrence Welk music wafted from a pair of wall speakers; the schmaltzy tunes mixed with the sounds of forks clicking on plates, of ice tinkling in glasses, and the crush of human conversations. Odors of frying fish drifted from the kitchen whenever its swinging door opened into the dining room.

The hostess seated Lane and me at a window table for two, with a view of the pass and the bridge. After we hung our jackets on our chair backs, we studied menus, bathed in the glow from a table lamp. The lamp's shade had a nautical motif on it: a mix of anchors and sea ropes and lanterns. I felt very grown up, sitting there with Lane and knowing I was treating him to a meal, just like normal guys did on dates with their girlfriends.

I was still deciding what I might order when I heard a woman's voice speak my name, and when I looked up, Mrs. Corrigan was standing by our table with a purse in her hand. She looked thinner than the last time I'd seen her, but she still looked nice in her dress and pearls. Her face was made up with lipstick and powder.

I stood to give her cheek a peck, then introduced her to Lane, who also rose to shake her hand.

"What a surprise to see you," she said while her gaze flitted back and forth between me and Lane. "I talked Kevin into coming here tonight, since he didn't have plans." Then she pointed across the room. "Our table's right over there."

Kevin sat in a corner booth. He wore a sports jacket over a white shirt and tie, and he buttered a roll with a knife. Even from across the room, I could tell he wasn't happy to be where he was. His chin was lowered and his mouth was a thin line.

I turned to Lane. "I'm going to say hi. I'll be right back."

When I approached the Corrigans' table with Kevin's mom, Kevin looked up, and as soon as he saw me, he gathered his eyebrows. He looked into my face and narrowed his eyes.

"Look who's here," Mrs. Corrigan said.

I raised a palm. "Hey, Kevin," I said while I shoved both my hands into the hip pockets of my chinos.

"What are you doing here?" he asked, as though I should be anywhere *but* the Kingfish Restaurant.

I jerked a thumb over my shoulder. "Lane and I are having dinner."

Kevin glanced over at Lane. Then he looked back at me, and when he did, his gaze lighted on my shirt pocket. After he studied the monogram there, he raised an eyebrow. "Whose shirt is that?"

"It's Lane's. I didn't have a fresh one to wear out, so he loaned me this."

Kevin didn't say anything; he just stared into my face with his eyes narrowed.

"Look," I said, "I need to go; I just wanted to say hi."

"Enjoy your dinner," Mrs. Corrigan said, and I turned on my heel without saying another word. Everything around me turned into a blur as I made my way back to our table, and when I got there, Lane looked at me funny.

"Your face is as pale as an egg," he said. "What's wrong?"

After I sat down, I shook my head. "I can't believe they're here tonight, and at just the same time we are. How could my luck be any worse?"

Lane crinkled his nose. "Why do you care if Kevin and his mom are here?"

I pointed to my chest. "He noticed your monogram; he asked whose shirt it is."

"So?"

"You don't understand: more than once he's asked if you and I fool around when I spend time with you. I've always told him no, but now you and I are out together at a restaurant and we're all dressed up. Kevin's not stupid; he's going to know I lied to him."

Lane shrugged. "Maybe it's about time he knows he has competition. He might treat you with more respect if he does."

I chewed my lips while I studied my menu. Maybe Lane was right. What was I gaining by hiding my relationship with Lane from Kevin?

We ordered our food. Lane chose fried flounder, and I picked red snapper stuffed with crabmeat. The meals came with salads and baked potatoes, and the food was tasty. But I couldn't help glancing over at the Corrigans from time to time, to see how Kevin was behaving. More than once, I caught him staring in our direction with a scowl on his face.

He knows.

Kevin and his mom left the restaurant before we did, and they didn't say good-bye before they did so, which was fine with me. Once they were gone, I could finally relax, even to the point of sharing a piece of pie with Lane.

After dinner, we strolled along the docks where commercial fishing boats were tethered for the night. The briny scent of moving Gulf water was strong in the air. Boats rocked and their lines squeaked. Above us, a three-quarter moon glowed while hundreds of stars twinkled in the cloudless night sky.

"Dinner was great," Lane told me. "Thanks so much."

I nodded. "Sorry if I seemed a little distracted. It's just that Kevin—"

Lane groaned. "Forget about him, will you? This is *our* weekend, and he shouldn't intrude on it."

"You're right," I said, then glanced at my wristwatch. "It's only nine thirty. Do you want to go someplace?"

"Like where?"

I thought for a moment. Then I said, "Do you like to bowl?"

"Heck, yeah. Let's do it."

A half hour later, we were lacing up our shoes at a bowling alley in South Pasadena, not all that far from where our high school was located. The place was packed with kids our age, mostly boy-girl couples on dates. The rumble of heavy balls rolling down twenty hardwood lanes mixed with the crash of tumbling pins. A gaggle of boys gathered about four pinball machines that made ringing noises when their lights flashed. Cigarette smoke hung in the place like a stage scrim.

Lane, of course, bowled gracefully, and I loved watching him dance toward the foul line with his ball hanging from his fingertips. Each time, he released the ball so closely to the lane's surface that the ball barely made a sound when it landed. His aim was deadly, and I quickly realized I wouldn't stand a chance of beating him no matter how many games we rolled. But I didn't care. Wasn't it enough that I was with Lane and I had him all to myself? How lucky could a guy get?

Of course, we couldn't show any real affection toward each other in the bowling alley, but when one of us rolled a strike or picked up a difficult spare, the other guy could show his approval with a shoulder squeeze or a back slap, and every time we touched, I felt a sexual charge pass between Lane and me.

By the time we returned to the Davises', the time was close to midnight, and both of us were yawning. We extinguished all the outdoor Christmas lights, then went inside. By mutual agreement, we postponed sex until the next morning. Instead, after we undressed in Lane's bedroom, we crawled beneath the covers and held each other. The room's windows were open and the air entering from outside was cool. After Lane switched off the nightstand lamp, we lay in darkness. He ran his fingers through my hair and kissed the crown of my head. Off in the distance, an outboard engine hummed. The bay's salty aroma wafted into the room while Lane's breath tickled my cheek.

"It's been a great day," I said.

"It sure has. Everything felt so easy and so right, like it was all meant to happen. Why do you suppose that is?"

I didn't know what to say. I knew Lane was looking for some sort of declaration from me, a statement that something beyond friendship and sex was growing between us. But if I made that sort of statement, it would mean I was gravitating away from Kevin. Maybe Lane would expect me to end things with Kevin, and then what would I do?

"I think we get along really well," I said, "but we shouldn't rush things. Let's take it one step at a time."

"I'm not trying to pressure you," Lane said.

"I know that," I said, "but let me explain something: Kevin's been my boyfriend for a year and a half. Life's been hard on him lately, what with his dad passing and his knee injury, so I don't want to hurt him even more."

Lane's leg fuzz tickled mine when he shifted his weight. "You know what I think? If you broke things off with Kevin tomorrow, he'd just find someone else to use. That's the kind of guy he is, and you shouldn't worry so much about him 'cause he sure doesn't worry about you."

I lay there in the darkness, trying to decide whether Lane's view on Kevin was accurate. Was Lane trying to come between Kevin and me? Or was he simply telling me truths about Kevin that I needed to face?

I SPENT SUNDAY morning at Lane's. We ate cornflakes in the kitchen, then bundled up. Our breaths steamed in the chilly air while we sat on Lane's dock, squinting in the brilliant morning sunshine that warmed our shoulders and made the bay glimmer like a mirror. We sat close enough that our shoulders and hips touched. A sailboat chugged by with its sails furled and its diesel engine clanking.

"I hate to see you leave so early," Lane said. "Are you sure you can't stay through the afternoon?"

I nodded. "I have a ton of homework due tomorrow, plus we have that test in Trig this week. I'll need to study for it."

Lane bobbed his chin. "Got plans for next weekend?"

I pursed my lips while I watched a dozen brown pelicans fly over us in V-formation. "Kevin will probably want to stay at my place since I didn't spend time with him this weekend, but I don't know that for certain. He's probably mad at me right now, so I might not even hear from him."

"I'd like to see you if possible," Lane said. "It doesn't matter when."

I nodded and said, "I'll do my best."

When it came time for me to go, Lane and I kissed in his foyer for at least ten minutes before he walked me out to my car, and I hoped none of his neighbors noticed the bulge in my jeans when he did so.

After I climbed into the Dart, Lane leaned on the sill of the driver's door. He looked in at me and moistened his lips. "If you get a chance tonight, take a few minutes and give me a call. I'll be missing you, so hearing your voice would make me feel a whole lot better, okay?"

"Of course," I said. "I'll do that."

While I backed the Dart out of Lane's driveway I felt a hollowness in the pit of my stomach, as though I were rapidly descending in an elevator. My eyes itched and I felt short of breath, and then I wondered, as I waved good-bye to Lane, if I was falling in love with him. Already I missed him terribly, and knowing how he felt about me made me wonder if I'd be an idiot not to commit myself to him.

And then I recalled what Lane had said about Kevin the night before.

"You shouldn't worry so much about him 'cause he sure doesn't worry about you."

Chapter Nineteen

MONDAY AFTERNOON, AT the end of classes, I met with my guidance counselor, Carmen Valenti, a stout woman known for her flaming-red hair, muumuu dresses, and Bakelite bracelets. We sat in her cramped and windowless office in my school's administration building. Overhead, a fluorescent ceiling fixture flickered and hummed. Valenti sat behind a wooden desk littered with file folders and educational publications. She spoke with a thick Brooklyn accent as she explained the federal government's student loan program.

"From what you've told me about your family's financial situation, I've no doubt you'd qualify for a loan. Your grades are excellent, and that makes you a good candidate for one of the state's universities, but you'll have to take the SAT in order to apply for admission."

I nodded, then told Valenti about the book Lane's folks had bought for me.

"That's good," Valenti said, "because preparing for the test can have a huge impact on your score. That's a statistical fact."

"How do I sign up for the test?"

Valenti's knees crackled when she rose. She opened a drawer in a file cabinet next to her desk and produced a registration form she handed to me. "Fill this out and return it to me, along with a check for eight dollars, payable to the testing service. The test will be given in the cafeteria on the second Saturday in April; that's the thirteenth."

I studied the form a moment or two, then looked up at Valenti. "But if I attend community college and live at home, I won't have to rack up so much debt. Maybe I shouldn't go to a university, at least not until after I earn my associate's degree."

Valenti closed her eyes and shook her head. Then she wagged a finger at my nose. "Don't let borrowing money spook you. Education's the best investment of time and money a young person can make. I'll get you a student loan application. You can pick it up when you drop off your SAT registration papers."

I nodded and, after thanking Valenti for her time, ambled down a school corridor while I pondered my future. Lane's parents *and* Mrs. Valenti seemed to think I'd be foolish to forgo a university education, but that would mean moving away from my mom and sister, *and* from Kevin. I'd have no beach to surf at. I'd lose my lawn-care business *and* I'd have to borrow a slew of money, something like eight thousand dollars. And something else: Lane had said the dormitories up in Gainesville looked like prisons, and I couldn't imagine myself living in one, much less taking my meals in a cafeteria. It seemed there were so many negative aspects to attending a university. Why should I go?

When I got home, Kevin sat in his Mustang on our driveway. He was smoking a cigarette and blowing smoke rings out his driver's door window. When I pulled the Dart alongside Kevin's car, he tossed the cigarette. He exited his car just as I left mine. He wore his Bishop Keating uniform, and despite his cane, he looked, as always, very sexy.

"What are you doing here?" I said.

He raised a shoulder, then let it drop. "I didn't see you all weekend," he said, "and I missed you, so can I come in?"

"Sure," I said, then I let us inside with a key.

As soon as we reached my room and I set down my books, Kevin wrapped his arms around my waist; he pulled me to him until our hips met, then brought his mouth to mine. While our tongues rubbed and our chin stubbles rasped, I tasted the cigarette he'd just smoked.

Kevin pulled his lips from mine. "Where's Lisa?" he asked, glancing here and there.

"She's rehearsing a school play."

He raised his eyebrows. "So we're alone?"

I nodded. "At least for an hour or so."

Kevin worked open a button on my shirtfront. "Why don't you lock the front door?"

Moments later, we kicked off shoes and unbuckled belts. Kevin seemed in a decent mood while we undressed, but right after I peeled off my undershirt, his gaze traveled to my collarbone, and then a vertical crease appeared between his eyebrows.

"What is that?" he said, pointing.

Uh-oh.

I couldn't hold Kevin's gaze, so I glanced out a window while I tried to think of what I should say.

Make up a story.

I looked back at Kevin. "We were out on Lane's boat Saturday. We hit a wave and I banged into the corner of the windshield. It's just a bruise."

Kevin grimaced and shook his head. "That's bullshit, Jesse. I know what a hickey looks like, so why are you lying?"

"I'm *not* lying, I—"

Kevin tackled me and drove me onto the bed. He fell on top of me, pinning me to the mattress. "Do you like it when your buddy chews on you?" he hollered. "Well, he's not here, but I am."

Kevin bit the side of my neck.

I winced while he sucked on my skin, but I didn't try to resist him. At that point, we wore only our briefs and I felt Kevin's erection rub against mine. I listened to his breath whistle in his nose while he kept on sucking. Minutes later, when he'd stopped, he dragged me to my feet and pushed me to my bureau mirror so I could view his handiwork. The hickey he'd fashioned was far larger than Lane's. It was brownish-red, perhaps the size of two silver dollars.

"Are you happy now?" Kevin said while holding both my arms at my sides. "Or would you like another?"

Before I could answer, Kevin ripped my briefs down to my ankles. He slapped my ass—hard. "Kick 'em off," he hollered. "Then get back on the bed."

I did as I was told, and Kevin followed me. After he seized a tube of jelly from my nightstand drawer, he yanked off his own briefs. Then he crawled atop me again. His hot breath steamed in my ear.

"I guess sex with me isn't enough?" he whispered. "You need it from your buddy too, and he likes it rough, is that it?"

When I didn't answer, Kevin kept on. "I can get rough too. Then maybe you'll feel more satisfied."

I didn't put up a fight. Kevin was stronger than me—he was angry as well—and I didn't want to provoke him any more than I already had. I just let him do as he pleased. He flipped me onto my stomach. Then he swatted my ass cheeks, over and over, until they stung like they'd been attacked by a swarm of bees. The pain actually brought tears to my eyes.

When he'd finished hitting me, Kevin had me kneel on the bed with the side of my face pressed to the mattress and my feet hanging over the edge. He lubed me with jelly, then took me from behind. It wasn't a rape; I never asked Kevin to stop. In fact, I didn't want him to because, in a weird way, it felt good to be punished for my infidelity.

After Kevin reached orgasm and withdrew from me, I rolled onto my back. Kevin lay beside me; he stared at the ceiling while his chest rose and fell. "I don't like hurting you," he said, "but I will if I have to. I won't share you with this Lane guy, and I can't stand the fact you let him touch you like that, especially after I let you screw *me*. I thought we were boyfriends."

"We are, but..."

"What?"

Go on: say it.

"You treat me like a light switch you can turn on and off whenever it suits you, and that's not fair. I have the right to expect something better."

Kevin turned his head to look at me. "And I guess that something better is Lane; is that what you're saying?"

I drew a breath, then let it out. "He treats me with respect," I said. "I'm not just a secret to Lane."

Kevin rose from the bed and strolled to a window. He stood there naked with his hands on his hips, staring into our backyard. I let my gaze travel over his sleek frame. I studied his buttocks and the muscles in his chest, shoulders, and arms. He was, without question, the most attractive male I'd ever met, and I knew I was probably an idiot for putting our relationship in jeopardy, but this time I wasn't backing down.

Kevin kept staring out the window while he spoke. "You have to make a choice," he said, "and I mean right now. It's either me or Lane; you can't have us both because I'm not sharing you with him. You're either mine completely or you're not at all."

I rubbed the fresh bruise on my neck. "I have an idea," I said. "Let's try being the kind of friends we *used* to be, back when we didn't touch each other. Maybe then we'll get along better."

When Kevin swallowed, I watched his Adam's apple bob. He still looked out the window while he responded to my suggestion. "That won't work for me. I don't want to be just friends; I need something more from you than that. So I guess this it. We're done."

Kevin reached for his briefs while my heart chugged. Would he really end things so abruptly? After all we'd been through, how *could* he? But he acted as though he were cancelling something as petty as a fast food order. For a moment—and I still can't believe this happened—I actually considered caving in to Kevin, but I didn't, not this time. I didn't because now I finally knew for certain that Kevin didn't give a shit about me. He only cared about himself and his own selfish needs.

"I'm sorry," I told him, "but I think you're right."

RIGHT AFTER KEVIN left, I phoned Lane and spoke of everything that had happened during the preceding hour.

Lane whistled when I'd finished. "Are you okay?"

"Not really," I said. "I'm pretty shook up. It'll be weird not having Kevin in my life; I feel bad about it, and I can't believe it's all over. Then there's the hickey he gave me today; it's huge. What'll I tell my mom and sister when they see it?"

Lane didn't answer right away, but when he did he said, "How about the truth?"

I gritted my teeth. "I don't know if I can do that."

"What choice do you have? They know you don't date girls, so how will you explain the marks on your neck? Will you tell them a dog bit you?"

I knew Lane was right; I'd have to spill the beans and I shook my head at the thought of doing so.

Shit.

My sister got home first. I managed to keep the hickey out of sight by staying in my room with the door closed, but then my mom came home, and when she hollered hello from the hallway, I knew it was time to talk. After all, I couldn't hide in my room for three days. For the tenth time, I checked my reflection in my bureau mirror. The T-shirt I wore did nothing to conceal the damage Kevin had done. The bruise had turned dark purple; it looked like an ugly tattoo.

I drew a deep breath. Then I strode into our living room where my mom read the newspaper and my sister studied a textbook. They both sat on our sofa. Already my heart pounded and my vision blurred. The room seemed to shrink when I cleared my throat. Both Mom and Lisa looked up at me with blank expressions on their faces.

"I have something to show you," I said, then I turned my head so both of them had a clear view of the hickey.

"Gross," my sister cried. "Who *did* that to you?"

I sat in our easy chair and rested my forearms on my knees. My gaze flitted between my sister and Mom. "Kevin did it," I said, "when he was here this afternoon. He's been my boyfriend ever since that summer he lived with us."

My sister's jaw dropped while my mother shifted her weight on the sofa. Neither of them said anything, so I kept on.

"I know you're both surprised, but I have to be who I am and I don't want to hide it from you any longer."

My mom asked, "Does Kevin's mother know about this?"

I shook my head.

My sister's gaze drilled into mine. "Do you and Kevin actually *do* stuff when he spends the night?"

I looked at her and nodded. "All the time."

Lisa rose and slapped the sides of both her thighs. "I can't *believe* this. You guys had sex while Mom and I slept right down the hall? That's disgusting and weird, and I can't *believe* my only brother's a homo. What could be worse?"

Lisa turned on her heel and stormed into the hallway leading to our bedrooms. Seconds later, her door slammed so loudly the house shook.

My mom crossed her legs at the knee. She clasped her arms in her hands. "Are you sure this is how you want to live your life? You don't want to marry and have children?"

I shook my head. "I know it sounds strange, but when I'm with another boy it feels very natural. I think it's what I was meant for."

Mom nodded. After she glanced toward my sister's room, she lowered her voice and spoke. "That summer Kevin stayed here, I heard noises coming from your room, several times, so I knew what you boys were up to."

"How come you didn't tell us to stop?"

Mom rocked her head from side to side. "You can't figure out what you want from life unless you explore your boundaries; it's how things work."

I nodded. "Are you disappointed in me?"

Mom reached for my forearm and gave it a squeeze. "Not at all, honey. I only want you to be happy, and if Kevin is what you *need* to be happy, then you should have him. Plus, you two have a friendship that goes back a long way."

I frowned. "There's a problem, Mom. I think my friendship with Kevin may have just ended."

My mother's eyebrows gathered. "What happened?"

I described my weekend with Lane, and how jealously Kevin had behaved about it. Then I talked about how Kevin had treated me over the past eighteen months. I even spoke of the night I went to the Bishop Keating dance.

Mom pursed her lips, then shared a little wisdom with me.

"A lot of men don't consider other persons' feelings when they act; they just bulldoze their way through life. Your father was that way and it destroyed our marriage. If you love a man like that and you want to keep him, then you have to accept his abuse because he will never change."

I nodded. "Every time Kevin hurt me, he always said he was sorry afterward. But then he'd hurt me again in exactly the same way. I think he's finally beaten my love for him to death. Can you understand what I'm saying?"

Mom closed her eyes and bobbed her chin. "Completely."

I cleared my throat, then pointed toward the hallway. "What about Lisa? I don't think she's handling this very well."

Mom shrugged. "You took her by surprise. Plus she's young and inexperienced. I'll have a talk with her; she'll get over it in time."

There in the living room, I suddenly felt as light as an oak leaf. Of course I was still saddened by Kevin's decision to dump me, but Mom's accepting me for who I was had lifted a huge emotional burden from my shoulders. I moved to the sofa and wrapped my arms around her.

After I gave her a hug, I said, "Thanks for understanding. You're the best mom a guy could ask for."

She looked at me and made a little smile. "You're not too shabby yourself, son."

Chapter Twenty

THE FRIDAY FOLLOWING my breakup with Kevin, Lane came to my house to have dinner and help us decorate our Christmas tree. The day before, I had described my relationship with Lane to my mom and sister.

"He's important to me," I told them, "so please make him feel welcome."

When Lane arrived, the four of us drank Cokes on our front porch while we chatted. Because darkness came early in December, I switched on a floor lamp and the glow from the lamp reflected in Lane's yellow hair. He looked handsome in an Oxford-cloth shirt, chinos, and penny loafers.

My mom asked Lane questions about his parents and what they did for a living. Lisa asked questions about the classes Lane took at school and if he planned on attending college. Lane answered patiently while Mom and Lisa sipped from their Cokes. My sister kept twirling strands of hair around her fingers while her gaze flitted back and forth between me and Lane, and I wondered if she thought Lane and I might paw each other at any moment. But of course we kept a respectable distance between ourselves.

Dinner was lasagna with a tossed salad and garlic bread. At the table, Lane asked my mom about her job and my sister about her school activities. As conversation flowed back and forth across the table, I sensed Mom and Lisa were warming up to Lane, especially when Lane talked about the bizarre street people who frequented the soup kitchen where he worked on Wednesday nights.

"A lot of them are mentally ill. One guy thinks he's Abraham Lincoln; another thinks he's an astronaut. One woman carries all her possessions in a shopping cart. We call her the Wig Lady because she wears a different wig every time she visits. She's asked me out three different times."

Lisa's eyes bugged. "What did you say?"

Lane shrugged. "I told her I was too young to date."

Everybody laughed.

My mom and sister cleaned up the kitchen while Lane and I carried tree decorations and light strands down from the attic. We brought those to the living room where our blue spruce perched in a metal stand. The night was chilly, so we got a blaze going in the fireplace. Then Lane and I tested each light strand; we replaced any burned-out bulbs with new ones. By the time Mom and Lisa had finished their kitchen work, Lane and I had already put the lights on the tree.

Mom served mugs of hot cider, and then all four of us went to work, hanging bulbs and tinsel. Several times, while we trimmed the tree, I noticed Lisa or Mom looking at Lane, and I tried to imagine what they were thinking when they did so. Were they sizing him up? Were they expecting some sort of abnormal behavior from Lane?

When the time approached eleven p.m., Lane told Mom and Lisa goodnight, and then I walked him to his VW. In the shadows on our driveway, we leaned against the VW's front fender and held hands while we talked.

"Your mom and sister are nice," Lane said.

"I just hope they didn't make you feel uncomfortable with all their questions."

He shrugged. "How else would they get to know me?"

We kissed for five minutes or so, and then Lane drove away with his muffler putt-putting while I stood at the curb with my hands in my pockets, watching his taillights fade. I savored the memory of Lane's lips pressed to mine and the feel of his tongue exploring my mouth.

Back inside, I found my mom and sister seated on the sofa. They stared dreamily at the fireplace and our brightly lit tree, but when I sat down in the easy chair, they both turned their gazes to me.

"Well," I said, "what do you two think?"

Mom crinkled her forehead, feigning confusion. "About the tree?"

I turned down one corner of my mouth. "I mean *Lane*."

"He sure is cute," Lisa said.

Mom looked at Lisa and rolled her eyes. Then she returned her gaze to me. "He seems very nice," she said, "and I can tell he likes you."

"How?" I asked.

Mom raised an eyebrow. "From the way he looks at you when you're talking. He hangs on every word you say."

SCHOOL LET OUT for Christmas break on December twenty-second, a Friday. Lane and I celebrated by going ice-skating at the Bayfront Arena in downtown St. Petersburg. The indoor rink was nearly the size of a football field where a mix of families with kids and teens on dates thronged. Everyone wore blue jeans and sweaters because the air inside the building was frigid.

I had never ice-skated, but Lane knew how because he'd once lived in Virginia for a year. "It's not hard," he told me while we laced up our rented skates. "The hardest part is turning."

I, of course, was completely helpless when I stepped onto the ice. But in a way, my clumsiness was an asset because it meant Lane had to hold onto my waist as I stumbled along ahead of him. I kept getting passed by little kids who looked like they'd been born on ice as they zoomed along. I must've fallen a half-dozen times. Each time, Lane caught me in his arms. Then he pulled me back upright while both of us laughed at my incompetence.

At one point, I told Lane I wanted to rest, and while I leaned against the rink's barrier wall, Lane cruised around the ice like a guy you might see in the Olympics. He made skating look effortless as he glided past me with his blond hair fluttering about his shoulders.

After an hour or so, we both took a break. We stepped off the ice and clunked across a rubber-matted floor to buy Cokes from a vendor. Then we found a bench where we could talk without anyone hearing us.

"I stink at skating," I told Lane. "Maybe it's a sport I'm not meant for."

Lane shrugged. "It's your first time; you're doing fine."

I sipped from my paper cup, savoring the Coke's fizzy sweetness. I watched couples skate together with smiles on their faces. Then I looked at Lane. "This is nice. It's like we're on a date again, isn't it?"

He looked at me and smiled. "A few days ago, I told my parents about us; I hope you don't mind."

I sucked air into my lungs while I raised my eyebrows. I tried to imagine the expressions on the Davises' faces at the moment Lane sprang the news on them. "What did they say?"

"They're fine with it; they like you."

I let out my breath. "Well, that's good."

"They want you to go to church with us on Christmas Eve. The service is at eight p.m., if you can make it."

Lane's invitation sent a quiver through me. Not only did his parents know we were boyfriends, but it seemed they actually *approved* of the relationship. How could life get any better?

"I'll need to check with my mom," I said. "If she says it's okay, then I'll be there."

SATURDAY MORNING, I drove to downtown St. Petersburg where I visited Maas Brothers, the area's nicest department store. It was tough finding a parking spot on the street. The sidewalks teemed with holiday shoppers toting shopping bags. The day was cool and sunny, and I wore a sweater and blue jeans. A light breeze tickled my cheeks as I strode toward the retailer. A woman in a blue Salvation Army uniform rang a bell at a corner while people passing her dropped coins into her bucket.

Inside the store, I had to snake my way through a crowd, brushing against people's shoulders like a running back avoiding tacklers. Christmas music wafting from loudspeakers mixed with the crush of five hundred human voices. I passed a perfume counter where bewildered male shoppers sniffed from bottles. The perfume scents were so strong they made me light-headed. The young men's clothing department was on the second floor, so I rode the escalator up there, right behind a smartly dressed woman who held a little boy's hand. The boy chattered away about visiting Santa Claus; he held a wish list in his free hand.

It didn't take me long to find what I wanted to buy Lane: a hooded sweatshirt with a logo from the surfing film, *The Endless Summer*. The logo featured silhouettes of three surfers on a beach with their boards while a huge yellow sun loomed in the background. I tried on a medium shirt, but it felt pretty tight on me, so I went with a large. I asked the saleslady for a gift box, then moved on. I bought my mom a nice pair of house slippers, and my sister an Aretha Franklin album, *I Never Loved a Man the Way I Love You,* which included Franklin's huge hit, "Respect."

After I toted my purchases to the Dart, I cruised westward on First Avenue North while wind rushed through the car and the radio played songs from the Beatles album, *Sgt. Pepper's Lonely Hearts Club Band.* My thoughts turned to Kevin Corrigan, and I wondered just how he and his mom would celebrate Christmas. I thought of the previous

Christmas, when Kevin had paid me a surprise visit in his new Mustang, and then I remembered our quarrel when Kevin took me for a ride and I exploded in anger at him.

In a sense, that quarrel in Kevin's Mustang had been the beginning of the end to my relationship with Kevin, even though it took me another year before I finally allowed it to halt. And what a painful year it had been. For twelve more months, I had endured Kevin's on-and-off neglect of my needs, but not now, not any longer.

I hadn't heard anything from Kevin since the day we broke up, and I wasn't expecting any calls or visits from him in the future. He'd given me an ultimatum, I had made my choice, and now I served no purpose to him. Why would he stay in touch?

Chapter Twenty-One

SUNDAY NIGHT WAS Christmas Eve. Right after my sister and I finished the dinner dishes, I dressed in my best outfit: white Oxford-cloth shirt, charcoal dress slacks, regimental necktie, penny loafers, and my sports jacket with brass buttons.

The sky was dark when I arrived at the Davises', and already their exterior Christmas lights glowed. I gave the illuminated Santa on the roof a little salute just before I rang the doorbell. Lane's dad answered the door with a smile on his face. He wore a business suit.

"Merry Christmas," he told me while we shook hands, and then I followed him inside.

I greeted Lane's mom, who wore a cardigan sweater over a silk blouse, a pleated skirt, and heels. She gave me a hug and a peck on the cheek. "We're so glad you could join us tonight. Every year, our church puts on a special Christmas Eve service; I think you'll enjoy it."

"Lane's in his bedroom," Mr. Davis told me. "I guess you already know where that is?"

I blushed while I nodded, then ambled down the hallway. I found Lane seated on his bed, polishing a penny loafer. He was dressed much like me, only his jacket was draped over his desk chair. Right away, he put down his shoe and rose. He held his arms out, and I slipped between them. After I put my arms around him, we kissed for a minute or so. Lane's tongue rubbed against mine while our lips smacked.

After Lane pulled his mouth from mine, he gave me a wink. "We'd better cut out the slobbering," he said, "or I'll walk into church with a stiffy in my pants."

I chuckled while I let my gaze travel about the room. I recalled the weekend I'd spent with Lane at his home and all the things we'd done in his bed. I remembered sleeping next to him and waking up to find him pressed up against me each morning.

"You look great," he told me.

Fresh blood rushed to my cheeks. I'd never had my appearance complimented by another boy, and the fact Lane found me attractive made me feel like someone special. How come Kevin had never told me I looked good?

We rode to church in the Davises' Oldsmobile 98, a massive sedan with leather upholstery. You could have fit five adults in the backseat, where Lane and I rode. As soon as Mr. Davis backed out of the driveway, Lane reached for my hand and held it during the drive to church. My heart thumped at the feel of his warm palm touching mine while we cruised eastward on Fifth Avenue North.

I hadn't been in a church in four years, not since my mom decided I needn't attend unless I wanted to. I preferred sleeping late on Sundays, so I quit going and, to be honest, my faith had wavered lately. In my mind, if God was truly running the show, he was doing a lousy job of it, what with the Vietnam War and the race riots in our inner cities. And he wasn't doing much to help my family either. Whatever we had—and that wasn't much—we'd earned through hard work, not His generosity.

Still, as we entered Lane's church, a peaceful feeling crept into me. An organist played "It Came Upon a Midnight Clear" while a stooped and gray-haired usher handed each of us a program for the service. The sanctuary's ceiling was vaulted. Wooden pews fanned out to either side of the carpeted aisle we walked down. Folks of all ages occupied the pews, and everyone wore dress clothes, even little kids. The altar with its brass cross was decorated with Christmas tree bows and red candles that gave off a warm glow. A pulpit to the right of the altar was draped in evergreen garlands and red fabric, and the choir chancel behind the altar was similarly adorned.

Lane and I followed his parents to a pew about six rows from the altar. Then all four of us sat, with me positioned between Lane and his mom, and in a way, I felt like I was *part* of the Davis family instead of just a tagalong. The fact that Lane's folks had asked me to join them at church on Christmas Eve wasn't something I took lightly. I figured their invitation was a signal that my relationship with Lane sat well with them.

The service began with a black-robed choir's entrance from two doors on either side of the chancel. They sang "Hark! The Herald Angels Sing" as they filed to their seats and the organ pumped. A youthful-looking minister, also wearing a black robe, ascended to the pulpit. Everyone stood while this occurred, and when the song ended, the minister asked everyone to take a seat. After a few introductory remarks by the minister, two dozen children, all of them grade-schoolers, filed into the sanctuary. They stood before the altar, and a choral director led them in singing "Oh, Little Town of Bethlehem."

Lane leaned toward me to whisper in my ear. "I used to be in the kid's choir when I was younger," he said. "We did this every Christmas."

I brought my lips to Lane's ear. "I'll bet you looked cute up there."

He rolled his eyes and shook his head.

The service didn't last all that long, maybe an hour. I enjoyed the music immensely, but I also liked the sermon. It differed so from the ones I'd heard every Sunday for years at our Methodist church. The minister at Lane's church emphasized the importance of family and friendships, of compassion, understanding, and forgiveness. There was no mention of sin or guilt or penitence. The minister even cracked a few jokes that made everyone laugh. Twice the entire congregation rose to sing, and it felt so nice sharing a hymnal with Lane while the two of us butchered "Silent Night."

When the service ended, we returned to the Davises', where Lane and I shed our jackets and loosened our neckties. Lane's mom served hot chocolate and Christmas cookies in the living room, and if a stranger had seen us at that moment, he'd probably have assumed we were just a normal family sharing Christmas cheer.

In between munches, I told Lane's parents how I'd signed up for the SAT. "I've already started using the preparation manual you gave me; I know it'll help."

"That's good," Lane's dad said while crossing his legs at the knee. "Any thoughts on where you'll apply for admission to college?"

"Not really," I said.

Mr. Davis looked at his wife, then returned his gaze to me. "I attended the University of Florida, as did Lane's mom. It's a fine—"

"Dad," Lane said with an annoyed tone in his voice, "it's Christmas Eve, so will you please let Jesse enjoy it? Save the career talk for another time."

Mr. Davis shrugged. "It's never too early to start planning those sorts of things. Next thing you know, you boys will graduate from high school."

I glanced back and forth between Lane and his dad. I didn't know what to say, so I kept my mouth shut.

Lane changed the subject. "I have an idea," he told me. "I hear the surf in Brevard County's good in late December. After Christmas, why don't we drive over? We can get a room like last time."

"Sounds good," I said.

Mrs. Davis rearranged her limbs while she moistened her lips. Her gaze traveled from her husband to me, and then to Lane. "Honey," she said to Lane, "not to intrude on your privacy, but..."

"What?" Lane said after he swung his gaze to her.

Mrs. Davis clasped her arms in her hands while she moistened her lips a second time. "If you and Jesse rent a motel room, how many beds will the room have?"

I lowered my chin while my cheeks flamed. When I glanced up at Lane, he was scowling at his mom. "Why are you asking me that?" he said to her.

Mrs. Davis looked at her husband before she returned her gaze to Lane. "Because your dad and I are entitled to know what you and Jesse do when the two of you are alone. We trust you, but still..."

Lane's dad spoke up. "You and Jesse aren't adults yet."

"And we're not kids, either," Lane said while he looked back and forth between his parents. "I can't believe you're even bringing this up, especially on Christmas Eve when Jesse's here."

"It's okay," I said to Lane. "I don't mind."

"Well, *I* mind," Lane said to me, then turned back to his parents. "I told you about me and Jesse because I assumed you'd *respect* our privacy. We haven't done anything I'm ashamed of, and if we choose to share a bed in Cape Canaveral, that's our business, not yours."

"Look," I said to Lane, "maybe I should leave."

Lane swung his gaze to me. "Please don't," he said. "Let's put our jackets on; we can sit on the dock for a while."

When I looked at Lane's parents, both of them stared at the carpet with blank expressions on their faces. They made no attempt to stop us from leaving, and within moments, we sat side by side in the chilly night air, bathed in the glow from the dock's Christmas lights.

"I'm *so* sorry about that," Lane said. "They had no business saying what they did, not with you there; how embarrassing."

"They're just being parents," I said.

"*Nosy* parents."

I told Lane about my conversation with my mom, when she'd told me about hearing Kevin and me having sex in my bedroom. "But she didn't interfere with what we were doing; she let it go on."

Lane shook his head. "I can't imagine *my* folks doing that."

I shrugged. "Mom thinks I *should* explore my sexual side so I can find out exactly what makes me happy."

Lane's jaw sagged when he looked at me. "She said that?"

I nodded.

"Can I move in with you?" Lane said. "Your house sounds like a *lot* more fun than mine."

We both laughed, and I asked Lane if I could see him the next day. "I bought you a present, and I want to give it to you. It won't take long."

"I'll come to your place," Lane said. "What's a good time?"

We agreed on two p.m., and then I said, "It's getting late; I should go."

Back inside, I wished Lane's parents a Merry Christmas while shaking Mr. Davis's hand and sharing a hug with Lane's mom. Then Lane walked me to my car. The glow from the Davises' Christmas lights bathed us in shades of yellow, red, and green. There wasn't a shadow to be found anywhere, but after he glanced here and there, Lane planted a big wet kiss on my lips. The kiss made me feel weak in the knees.

"Merry Christmas, Jesse," he whispered. "I love you."

Chapter Twenty-Two

CHRISTMAS MORNING, I woke to the sound of a stiff breeze stirring the fronds on a Sabal palm outside my bedroom window. The sun was up but obscured by a bank of cirrus clouds that looked like tattered tissue paper strewn across the sky. Already my mom banged pots and pans around in the kitchen and the aroma of brewing coffee stole into my room. I dressed in jeans, a flannel shirt, and house slippers, then visited the bathroom. My hair was a hopeless mess of tangles and my eyes looked puffy. I splashed my face with cold water and did my best to brush my hair into place while shaking my head. Would Lane still love me if he saw me right now?

At Mom's request, I started a blaze in our fireplace while Mom and my sister prepared our traditional Christmas breakfast: scrambled eggs with bacon, grits, and cinnamon rolls. The scents wafting from the kitchen made me salivate.

I used a poker to rearrange flaming logs while my thoughts turned to the previous evening at Lane's and also to the words exchanged between Lane and his parents just before he and I left for the dock. Was *my* mom wondering what Lane and I did when we were alone?

Over breakfast, I spent a good deal of time describing the Christmas Eve service at Lane's church. My mom and sister had also attended a service at the Methodist church my mom belonged to, but when she described it, the service sounded far more formal than the one I'd gone to.

After we finished our meal and cleared the table, we gathered in the living room to exchange our gift-wrapped presents. My sister and mom had pooled their money to buy me a joint gift, something I'd told them I wanted. It was a bomber-style jacket much like the one I'd borrowed from Lane the day we visited Egmont Key, a light suede model with a zippered front, banded cuffs, and a banded waist. The size they'd chosen fit my lanky frame just right, and the suede was so soft I couldn't help but stroke it with my fingertips while I watched my sister and mom open their gifts.

I suppose most folks would have considered my family's Christmas a modest one. Besides the jacket, my only other gifts were stocking stuffers: underwear, socks, and a new wallet. But I didn't feel the least bit deprived. We were together—my mom, my sister, and I—and we were getting through life without anyone's help. I took great pride in that, and I wondered what my disappearing dad might say if he could see us just then.

Was he even celebrating Christmas? And did I even care?

My sister and I did the breakfast dishes; we cleaned the frying pan and coffeepot. We wiped down the kitchen counters and the stovetop, and we put things away. Lisa still wore her nightgown and slippers and her hair was tousled from sleep, but she looked cute nonetheless. We chatted while we worked, and somewhere during our conversation, Lisa asked me about Kevin.

"Mom said you broke up with him. Is that right?"

I nodded.

"Have you heard from him since?"

I shook my head. "I think our friendship's over. I'm not happy about it—I didn't want things to end completely—but Kevin said I had to stop seeing Lane or else he and I were through."

Lisa gathered her eyebrows. "He was that jealous?"

I grimaced and nodded.

Lisa chuckled while shaking her head.

"What is it?" I asked.

She shrugged while hanging a coffee mug on a cup hook. "It's just...you gay guys aren't much different than boy-girl couples."

"How so?"

"Mom's told me how Kevin behaved toward you; I mean the neglect and all. I know girls whose boyfriends take them for granted the same way, and I always tell them, 'Why do you put up with it? Have a little self-respect.'"

I nodded while I emptied coffee grounds into the garbage can. "That's easy to say, but when you're crazy about a guy like I was about Kevin, then you can't bear the thought of losing him. So you take his crap in exchange for keeping him in your life."

Lisa turned from her work. "You were that much in love with Kevin?"

I nodded. "So badly my stomach hurt when I couldn't see him."

Lisa lowered her gaze while she rubbed her lips together. Then she looked into my face again. "I'm sorry I called you a homo; it wasn't nice."

"It's okay, I—"

"No, it's *not* okay. You're my big brother and I'm proud of you, plus I think it's kind of cool how two super-cute guys want you so much. Most girls would *kill* to be in your shoes."

I couldn't help but laugh. "Thanks, Sis," I said, "but one guy at a time is enough for me."

Hours later, when Lane appeared at our house, I led him to our kitchen where Lisa and Mom prepared our Christmas dinner. Already the scent of roasting turkey filled the room. Lane wore a pale yellow sweater and corduroy jeans, and his blond hair brushed his shoulders. He greeted Mom and Lisa with an easy grin, and I suggested he and I take a walk to the shore.

"We'll have to bundle up," he said. "The wind's chilly out there."

In my room, I put on shoes and my new jacket. Lane retrieved his own jacket from his VW, and then we strolled westward while the breeze tossed our hair into our faces. We walked with our hands stuffed into our jacket pockets. The sun kept disappearing behind puffy cloud banks, and then everything around us would darken.

Lane rubbed the tip of his nose with a knuckle while he kept his gaze on the horizon. "I had a *serious* talk with my parents last night, right after you left. It lasted till midnight."

"Tell me what was said."

Lane pursed his lips and shook his head. "It wasn't pretty, but at least everyone was honest. We said what we had to."

"And?"

"I told them we've had sex multiple times. I said I wasn't going to apologize for it and we weren't going to stop. My mom started *crying*. She said she was afraid I'd catch some kind of disease or that maybe you might injure me when...you know."

"So they know what we're doing in bed?"

Lane nodded. "I told them, 'Look, if it'll make you feel better, Jesse and I will see a doctor for a checkup, so you'll know we're both healthy. And I promise we won't do anything harmful to each other. We're always gentle when we're together.'"

We walked in silence for a minute or so, until we reached the shore. The Gulf's hue was battleship gray; it churned like the inside of a washing machine. Angry waves made roaring sounds when they crashed onto the shore. The wind whistled in our ears, and we had to raise our voices to be heard above the din.

"They want to meet with your mom," Lane said, "along with you and me, so we can all agree on things."

"What kind of things?"

Lane rocked his head from side to side. "How often we'll see each other, and whether or not you can spend the night with me or vice versa. And then there's our trip to Cape Canaveral..."

"What?"

"They seem to think we'll spend the whole trip fucking. They want us to promise we'll behave while we're over there."

I made a face. "What does 'behave' mean?"

Lane rolled his eyes and shook his head. "Who knows? Look, do you think your mom would be willing to meet in the next few days? I know it's a lot to ask, but maybe if we all talk together, my parents will feel better about things."

"I'll ask her," I said.

Back at the house, we warmed our hands by the fireplace, and then I gave Lane his gift in my bedroom, *with* the door closed. He beamed when he held the sweatshirt before him. "It's so cool," he said, then kissed my cheek. "But now I feel terrible 'cause I didn't buy you a gift."

"It's okay," I said. "Being with you is the only present I need."

TWO DAYS AFTER Christmas, on a Friday evening, my mom and I sat in the Davises' living room with glasses of Coca-Cola resting on the coffee table before us. I wore school clothes, and my mom wore an outfit she'd worn to work that day. Lane and his parents sat across the table from us; they sipped from their own glasses while they listened to Mom compliment the beauty of their home, and I wondered how the Davises might feel if they saw *our* home and its modest furnishings.

Lane wore the *Endless Summer* sweatshirt I'd given him, along with a pair of blue jeans, and he looked so handsome I wanted to kiss him, right there in front of everyone. Each time his gaze met mine, a little shiver ran through my limbs.

The five of us traded small talk for ten minutes or so before Lane's dad cleared his throat. He leaned forward to rest his forearms on his knees, and then he looked at Mom. "Lane and Jesse plan to visit the east coast tomorrow; they want to rent a motel room for one night. Now that we all know how...*close* the boys are, Bev and I thought this meeting ought to happen."

"Yes," Lane's mom said while shifting her weight in her chair, "Lane's been frank with us about his private life with Jesse, and while we think Jesse's a fine young man, we're concerned."

"And not just about the boys' health," Lane's dad said, "but also about the propriety of what they're doing. I know times are changing. We're not in the fifties anymore, and it seems young people do whatever they please these days. Still..."

After Mom took a sip from her glass of cola, she returned the glass to the coffee table. Then she crossed her legs and placed both her hands atop her knee. She spoke to Lane's parents in an even cadence.

"Perhaps I have a different approach to parenting than you do," she said. "Jesse's father disappeared when Jesse was six. I raised my children on my own and I always worked full-time, so Jesse and his sister have enjoyed more freedom than most children. They're used to making their own decisions."

Lane's dad raised his eyebrows. "Do you approve of these boys having sex together?"

Mom blinked her eyes a few times before she answered. "Whether or not I approve isn't the issue here—not in my view—because what I think isn't going to change their behavior. They're sixteen years old, almost adults, and we can't follow them around all day long."

Lane's mom straightened her spine while her gaze drilled into Mom's. "Would you allow the boys to have sex under your roof? Is that what you're saying?"

I sucked in my breath, then held it. The room was as silent as an empty church. I glanced at Lane, but he wasn't looking at me. His gaze was fixed on my mom, just like his parents' were. No one moved a muscle when Mom spoke.

"I'll rely on Jesse and Lane to use their discretion, not just at your home or mine, but also in Cape Canaveral or wherever else they might be. I think we'll have to trust their judgment. I don't see that we have any other choice."

Lane's parents looked at each other for a long moment, and Lane's mom pursed her lips. "I suppose she's right," she told Lane's dad. "We can't control what they do when we aren't around, can we?"

Lane's dad shook his head, and then he turned to Lane.

"You boys be careful in Cape Canaveral."

Chapter Twenty-Three

ON A SATURDAY afternoon in mid-February, I wheeled my mower and edger down a neighborhood side street. I was headed home after tending three lawns. My muscles ached and my limbs felt tired, but I looked forward to spending an evening with Lane. He would have dinner with my family, and then he and I planned to see *Cool Hand Luke,* a Paul Newman film all the guys at school were crazy about.

The sky looked like dishwater. A chilly breeze blew from the northeast; I shivered in my oil-stained sweatshirt and holey blue jeans. A loose shoelace on my sneaker flipped here and there. I hummed a tune by the Turtles, "Happy Together," as I ambled along—I felt as contended as a cat on a sundrenched windowsill—but then I turned a corner and my heart leapt into my throat.

Holy shit, it can't be.

But it was. Kevin Corrigan's Mustang sat curb-parked in front of a house I knew quite well: it was Spencer's home. Right away, my eyes itched and my stomach roiled. In my mind's eye, I pictured what surely went on inside: a naked Kevin atop an equally naked Spencer; Kevin thrusting while the bedsprings sang and Spencer's sighs filled the room.

I felt like crying, and my reaction to the situation stunned me. I hadn't seen or spoken to Kevin in two months; I thought I'd put my breakup with him behind me, especially now that I had Lane in my life. But while I stood there on the road with my knees wobbling and my eyes fogged up, I knew better. We had a past, Kevin and I, going all the way back to the Jungle. He was my first friend and later my first lover. He knew every inch of my body and I knew every inch of his.

A jealous rage boiled up inside me. Kevin was with Spencer instead of me? How could it happen? I kneaded the handlebar of my mower while I stared at Spencer's house. Should I bang on the front door? Should I confront Kevin and let him know how ridiculous I found his behavior? Was he so desperate that he'd actually stooped so low? I thought of Spencer in his smock at the Rexall, smirking at me while I purchased the tube of jelly. I had felt a sense of pride when I turned down his invitation that day, knowing Kevin would spend the weekend at my house. But now Kevin lay in Spencer's bed, not mine, and Spencer was surely having the last laugh on me.

Let it go, Lockhart, I told myself while my chest rose and fell.

Just...turn away and go.

I trekked home to an empty house with my lips trembling and tears leaking from the corners of my eyes, but I didn't fall apart until I reached my room. I closed the door, then flopped facedown onto my bed. My trembling started in my shoulders; it worked its way through my body till even my hands and feet shook. I sobbed like a baby while scenes of my love life with Kevin played inside my head.

I recalled the night Kevin had first crawled into my bed. He'd opened a door for me; he had led me into a beautiful place I didn't know existed. I recalled the piney scent of Kevin's skin and the coconut aroma of the lotion we used as lubricant that night. Then I recalled the Fourth of July when we lay on a bedsheet in our sea oat atoll while fireworks exploded in the night sky. I'd never felt so close to another person as I did toward Kevin that summer. I had craved Kevin's flesh ever since that morning in his garage, way back in the Jungle, when I was eleven. So why should it surprise me that I still wanted him now? He was a narcotic I'd always be addicted to, no matter how hard I tried to resist the urge, and right now, I needed his touch, just like I needed air to breathe.

My stomach felt as if someone had plunged a knife into it, and now they were twisting the blade. My mouth tasted like it was full of pennies and the back of my throat burned. After sitting up, I seized a metal wastebasket alongside my bed and puked up a torrent of stinky green liquid; it splattered the walls of the basket like split pea soup.

I gasped for air while my brain churned. I felt as if I were reliving the day when Kevin had moved back to Largo after spending all summer with me. But this time was different because I had *chosen* to separate from Kevin. *I* had created the entire situation, and what a fool I'd been for doing so, what an *idiot*.

Go to him, I told myself. *Do it now.*

After I stumbled into the bathroom, I splashed cold water on my face and rinsed out my mouth. I dragged a brush through my tangled hair and straightened my clothing as best I could. I left the house with my hands balled into fists. The cold breeze hit my cheeks like a pair of slaps when I strode down the sidewalk toward Spencer's place.

I had no idea what I would do or say when I got there; I just knew I needed to see Kevin. I wanted to hear his voice, no matter what he might say to me when I appeared on Spencer's doorstep. And maybe, just maybe, if I promised Kevin I'd belong to him *and* that I'd never touch Lane again, Kevin would take me back and things would be as they once were.

Strangely, I felt almost giddy, like an inmate who's about to be released from prison. I broke into a run. My sneaker soles slapped the asphalt beneath me while the homes on either side of the street turned into blurs. My breath huffed and my lungs pumped when I turned the corner leading to Spencer's house. I felt so excited I thought my heart might burst from my chest, but then I reached Spencer's place and my spirits plunged like an anchor dropped into the ocean.

Kevin's Mustang was gone.

I froze in the middle of the street while all the energy I'd ginned up drained from me in an instant. I felt as empty and useless as a discarded shoe. There on the asphalt, I hung my head until my chin touched my sternum. I closed my eyes and flexed my fingers at my hips, but at least I didn't cry. I guess I'd already used up all the tears my body could muster that afternoon, so I only stood there breathing until a car horn tooted, and when I looked up, I realized I was blocking traffic. An old man behind the wheel of Chrysler New Yorker shook his fist at me while his lips formed angry words I couldn't hear.

I drew a breath, then let it out. After I stuffed my hands inside the front pockets of my jeans, I left the street. My feet felt as heavy as bricks when I shuffled homeward on the sidewalk.

I GUESS JEALOUSY can make a guy act stupid; he'll do things that don't make any sense in hindsight.

The afternoon I first saw Kevin's car at Spencer's, I acted *really* dumb. For several minutes, I forgot how badly Kevin had treated me when I was his boyfriend. I forgot his callous neglect of my needs. I forgot about that awful night at the Keating High School dance when Kevin had so cruelly put me in my place, and I even forgot about *Lane*, if that makes a bit of sense.

All I wanted was for Kevin to tell me I mattered more to him than anyone else. I'd have *killed* to hear those words from his lips. But hours later, when I sat at our dinner table, I savored the feel of Lane's knee resting against mine. I listened to the rise and fall of his voice, and knew Kevin would never be the right guy for me. He was someone I needed to bury in the same emotional graveyard I'd placed my father in.

There would be no more looking back, no more regrets, and no more second-guessing.

Good-bye, Kevin.

Chapter Twenty-Four

I'M NOT SURE how long Kevin's affair with Spencer lasted, but over the space of a few months I saw Kevin's Mustang parked at Spencer's house several times, so I know their fling lasted that long. In truth, I didn't care how long it continued because I didn't care about Kevin anymore. I had my life to live and a boyfriend who loved me without shame. Why waste time hoping Kevin might become something he never would?

I took the SAT in April, and my combined score placed me in the eighty-sixth percentile of all those tested. Lane scored almost as well— we both received letters of acceptance to the University of Florida in the spring of our senior year of high school—but being independent sorts, Lane and I chose a different path. Much to the disappointment of Lane's folks *and* Carmen Valenti, we enrolled at Brevard Community College in Cocoa Beach, where we attended classes with kids whose fathers worked for NASA or served at Patrick Air Force Base.

Lane and I rented one half of a furnished duplex in Cape Canaveral with a weed-and-dirt yard, no air-conditioning, and a beer-swilling carpenter named Wayne as our neighbor. A good surfing break was only two blocks from our front door, so after classes we could hit the water whenever waves were firing. Our apartment sat on the east side of the duplex, and each morning we woke to the cries of seabirds at the shore. We smelled the Atlantic's briny scent.

I brought my mower and edger to the Cape when we moved there, and it didn't take me long to build a customer base in our neighborhood. My earnings, combined with proceeds from a student loan, helped make ends meet.

I liked east coast living. An onshore breeze nearly always blew; it kept things comfortable even on the hottest of days. I liked our working-class neighbors and their lack of pretension, and I don't think they ever suspected what went on privately between Lane and me. To them, I suppose, we were just two college boys who liked to surf. Our two years in Brevard County flew by, and after we earned our associate degrees, we transferred to the University of Florida to earn our bachelors.

I can't say that I enjoyed landlocked Gainesville; I missed the sound of waves slapping a shore. But I earned an engineering degree there, Lane a degree in journalism, and then, after graduation, we returned to Pinellas County. We rented a cottage in Sunset Beach, only a few miles south of my mom's house on Treasure Island. Eventually, we bought the cottage from our landlord, and we have lived there ever since. Lane and I never made a lot of money in our respective careers, but we've done okay; the bills get paid.

There's actually a half-decent surfing break only a short distance from our house, and a few times each month, Lane and I will dust off our boards. Then we join all the teenagers and college kids on the lineup. We ride a few waves and remember the days when we could surf for hours and not get tired.

Lane and I have been a couple for almost fifty years, which I find pretty amazing. Of course Lane's put on weight and his hair has thinned, but he still looks beautiful to me when I wake next to him in the morning. Sometimes I rest my cheek against his warm shoulder. I listen to waves crash against the nearby beach and think about how lucky I am to have Lane in my life.

What more could a guy ask for?

I ONLY SAW Kevin Corrigan once after our breakup. When Lane and I came home for spring break from the university, during our junior year, my mother told me Kevin's mom had just died. Her funeral would take place at St. Jude two days hence. Mom asked if I would attend with her, and though I didn't want to go I said I would.

Kevin was only twenty-two at the time, but he looked older when he stood alone to greet a short line of mourners in the chapel foyer. He wore a rumpled business suit and a necktie, and he kept tugging at his shirt collar whenever he got the chance. His shoulders seemed to sag and the freckles on his nose had faded, but he still looked handsome with his blond hair, square chin, and twinkly blue eyes.

When Mom and I reached Kevin, his face lit up while his gaze traveled from Mom to me. He hugged my mother, then shook my hand while he thanked us for coming, and if he harbored any anger or resentment toward me, he didn't let it show. I think Kevin was genuinely glad to see us. We had probably known him longer than anyone else present, and in a sense we were all the family he had left.

When Mom asked Kevin what he was doing with his life, he explained that he lived with his girlfriend on Madeira Beach, where he helped crew a commercial fishing boat; it sailed weekly from the John's Pass Marina in search of grouper.

"I'm out in the Gulf for days at a time," he told us. "My girl doesn't like it, but the money's good and the guys on the boat are fun."

I'll bet they are, I thought while I studied Kevin's inscrutable visage. *I'll bet they are...*

NO PHOTOGRAPH ACCOMPANIED Kevin's obituary when I read it this morning. I suppose the *Times* charges extra for that sort of thing. But since today is Saturday, I took the time to leaf through pages of a photograph album I'd found at my mother's house several years ago, not long after she passed. The album was the kind with heavy black pages that mumbled when I turned them. The crinkly edged black-and-white snapshots in the album were held in place by little gummed corners Mom had carefully positioned on each page.

Most of the photos depicted me and my sister during various stages of our childhood and adolescence, but then I found one of Kevin and me, taken back in our Jungle days. We wore our hobo Halloween costumes. We had smudged our faces with burnt cork so we looked like we hadn't shaved in a week, and we stood before the Corrigans' front door with our arms draped across each other's shoulders.

We looked about as happy as two boys could be.

About the Author

Jere' M. Fishback is a former journalist and trial lawyer. He lives on a barrier island on Florida's Gulf Coast.

Website: http://www.jeremfishback.com

Also by Jere' M. Fishback

Tyler Buckspan
Becoming Andy Hunsinger (Coming Soon)

Coming Soon from Jere' M. Fishback

Becoming Andy Hunsinger

It's 1976, and Anita Bryant's homophobic "Save Our Children" crusade rages through Florida. When Andy Hunsinger, a closeted gay college student, joins in a demonstration protesting Bryant's appearance in Tallahassee, his straight boy image is shattered when he's "outed" by a TV news reporter.

In the months following, Andy discovers just what it means to be openly gay in a society that condemns love between two men. Can Andy's friendship with Travis, a devout Christian who's fighting his own sexual urges, develop into something deeper?

Also Available from NineStar Press

www.ninestarpress.com

www.ingramcontent.com/pod-product-compliance
Lightning Source LLC
Chambersburg PA
CBHW022124170626
46808CB00002B/830